FEAR IN FAIRHOPE

A Bremen and Whitacre Murder Mystery

FEAR IN FAIRHOPE

A Bremen and Whitacre Detective Agency Mystery

M.W. Burdette

ISBN-13: 9798649686761

Original Publication Date: 2021. Published in the United States of America by Amazon.com.

For the Fairhope Mafia

CONTENTS

Prologue

PART I: AN HISTORIC TOWN

The Pretty Town of Fairhope

Checking out the Town

Meeting with the Mayor

Initial Background Checks

The Broken Silence

Fingerprints Don't Lie

Boots on the Ground

The Plot Thickens

The Back Door

The Autopsy

PART II: A DOMESTIC NIGHTMARE

A Hidden Agenda

Setting the Trap

A Wolf in Sheep's Clothing

Moving Parts

The Master Plan

The Revelation

Ben Franklin's Help

Mayor Jackson

Vanishing Evidence

Epilogue

Prologue

Famous for its "jubilee," a natural phenomenon which occurs on the shores of the small city, when flounder, crabs and shrimp swarm in high density along the shallow bay, Fairhope is a fisherman's paradise. Residents and visitors alike boast of Fairhope's famous fish gathering traditions that occur with annual regularity along the water's edge. Buckets of live fish can be swept up and gathered without the need for fishing lines and fishing nets by anyone brave enough to wade into the calm backwaters of Mobile Bay when the jubilee occurs. There are only two places on the face of the Earth where jubilees occur—Tokyo Bay in Japan and the eastern shores of Mobile Bay in Baldwin County, Alabama. In Baldwin County there may be several small jubilees, or there may be one massive one, with them usually taking place in the summer months of the year.

According to researchers at Auburn University, for a jubilee to take place, a very specific set of conditions must exist. They usually only occur in the summer in the morning before sunrise. The previous day's weather conditions must include an overcast or cloudy day, a gentle wind from the east, and a calm and slick bay surface. Also, a rising tide is necessary; a change to a falling tide will stop the jubilee. It takes a combination of all these conditions to produce the phenomenon.

Jubilees are caused primarily by upward movement of oxygen-poor bottom waters forcing bottom-type fish and crustaceans ashore. Bottom water low in oxygen results from several coincidental circumstances, pockets of salty water accumulate in the deep parts of the northern portion of Mobile Bay stagnate during calm conditions. The stagnation is caused by salinity stratification, or layering effect, with the heavier salty Gulf water overlain by lighter, fresher river water. Stratification prevents movement of oxygen from the air into the bottom saline water. There are signs that a jubilee might occur, but the phenomenon happens almost instantaneously. By the time the casual observer is notified of the occurrence, it is almost over. Many times, the event lasts for less than an hour, making it possible for those present to gather unlimited amounts of fish and crustaceans, put them into large buckets and barrels, and rush home with their bounty from the sea.

The motto for Fairhope is "You've Arrived!" and that says something about the public relations message the city fathers want to send to everyone who passes through their artsy city. Small ethnic cafes, art galleries, open-air coffee shops, and small, home-owned retail shops dot the landscape of this small town. Fairhope is also home to a couple of boat harbors, as well as a first-class golf course and county club.

Rocky Creek Golf Club had been designed by Earl Stone with every golfer in mind, the unique characteristics separating this course from others. Rocky Creek is a must play when you are on the Gulf Coast. It was established in 1993. The club is located in Fairhope, Alabama on the Eastern Shore of Mobile Bay. This 18-hole 7,000-yard championship course is dramatically designed to create a challenge for both the amateur and the professional. Rocky Creek is truly one of the top courses located along the Gulf Coast. The golf course is surrounded by an upscale housing development of over 400 homes, many of them the largest and best landscaped properties in the State of Alabama.

While Rocky Creek Golf Club was not at the level of the Augusta National Golf Club, the world-famous course in Augusta, Georgia, where the U.S. Masters is played every spring, Rocky Creek was one of the top public golf courses in the State of Alabama. It was not uncommon for a member of Rocky Creek to see a famous professional golfer eating a sandwich in the restaurant or drinking a beer at the 19th Hole Lounge. It was considered to be poor manners to approach such a player and ask for an autograph in the formal dining area, but it was still done at times.

* * *

Spring had turned to summer in Ashburn, and summer was turning to fall, with the leaves beginning to fall and the color of the magnificent hardwood trees on the Quad across the street showing off their reds, oranges, and yellow foliage. Julie had decided not to return to college in the fall to seek a law degree, and she was becoming a very integral part of the John Bremen Detective Agency. Daphne and John promised to include her some on their next serious case, letting her get some field time and experience under her belt. As they sat rocking in their chairs, Julie heard the telephone ringing in the office.

"Just a minute. I'll be back. Does anyone want their drink refreshed while I am up?" Everyone shook their heads. They just want to sit, sip their drinks, and take in the beauty of a perfect, fall day. Julie came back with the portable phone in her hand. "You'd better take this, John," she said, handing him the receiver. He put the call on speaker phone, and they all listened to the person on the other end of the line.

"John Bremen?" a man's voice asked. "Are you John Bremen?"

“I am. Who’s asking?” John replied.

“This is Mayor Todd Jackson of Fairhope, Alabama. I want to speak to you about opening an investigation in our little town here in Baldwin County. Can you or some of your staff come to see me and discuss it with me soon? Time is of the essence.”

“Sure, Mayor. Maybe you can share just a little about why you chose our small agency to help you solve your problem.”

“Governor Big Jim Flowers suggested I call you.”

“OK, Mayor. What has happened to make things so necessary for expediency?”

“There has been an incident at Rocky Creek Golf Club here in Fairhope. Governor Flowers says you and your team are the best money can buy to help us with our problem.”

“And just what is that problem, Mayor?”

“Are you familiar with the name Larry Washington?”

“Larry Washington the PGA Champion?”

“The same. His body was found floating in a water trap this morning on the back side of the golf course, between the 13th and 14th hole. It looks like he was hit in the head with something resembling a golf club. We have the funds to pay your fees, so please tell me you’ll come and help us out.”

PART I: AN HISTORIC TOWN

Chapter 1

The Pretty Town of Fairhope

According to official historical records, Fairhope, Alabama, was founded in November 1894 on the site of the former Alabama City as a radical, utopian socialist, Georgist "Single-Tax" colony by the Fairhope Industrial Association, a group of 28 followers of economist Henry George who had incorporated earlier that year in Des Moines, Iowa.

Now that is definitely a mouthful of description about a small town that today refers to itself as a city where “You’ve Arrived!” For most residents living in this small, quiet coastal town one of the biggest daily questions was whether they would be going out for seafood for dinner, or who is cooking seafood at home. Shrimp was sold on street corners, in convenience stores, and in the large grocery store chains that dotted the landscape in shopping centers in every community. Fairhope had a population of approximately 15,000 residents, with an occasional influx of tourists and visitors that might total 2,000 at any one time of the year. Unlike Mobile, Alabama, her neighbor to the west across Mobile Bay, Fairhope was more of a town than a city. Sure, it had a legitimate police force, fire department, public works department, and public library, but there was space in Fairhope to live one’s life to the fullest. In Mobile the population was approaching 200,000, making Mobile the fourth largest city in the State of Alabama, bringing with that population more crime, congested highways, and unrest among the multi-ethnic neighborhoods. Many residents drove to Mobile to see medical specialists, to shop at nationally famous department stores, and to do other less ethical things that happen frequently in large metropolitan areas. There were prostitutes in Fairhope, for sure, but finding them would be more difficult than in a city like Mobile. Job opportunities in Mobile and the surrounding suburbs were exponentially greater than in the harbor town of Fairhope. More people thought of Fairhope as a place to retire, kick back, and enjoy the fruits on one's life of labor, not as a town that rarely sleeps. There were secret clubs and speakeasy bars that served their clientele 24/7, in violation of the city ordinances that were on the books in Mobile, although they were never really enforced. Mobile nightlife was more like Atlanta, New York, or Chicago, whereas Fairhope pretty much closed down around 11:00 PM. It wasn't Mayberry, but it was close.

Fairhope was more famous for the jubilee run of fish each year than anything else. There was a nice, professionally maintained country club and golf course, a public and private yacht club, and wonderful restaurants and cozy bars. However, there were not any real nightclubs where exotic dancers pranced around the stage attired in nothing but their G-strings, nor were there any gambling houses like in Biloxi, Mississippi, located just sixty miles to the west of Mobile. Fairhope was a healthier atmosphere in which to rear one's children, become involved in the Rotary Club or the Kiwanis, or own a small business in a community where everyone seemed to know everyone else.

Unlike many of the small seaport towns in South Alabama or Mississippi, Fairhope was a relatively new city, chartered in 1894, and well after Mobile was founded in 1702, and Naches, Mississippi, was established in 1740, both by the French. And, since it was founded after the Civil War, there weren't many years of conflict and war in and around Fairhope. That's what the residents liked about Fairhope—peace and tranquility. Anything that proved to upset those standards was looked upon with dread. Murders and personal attacks in Mobile, Birmingham, and Montgomery were always around 100 or more in each city per year, whereas Fairhope rarely recorded a murder at all. There was crime—robberies, assaults, theft-by-taking, and personal crimes that didn't rise to the level of murder—but many of those crimes could have been prevented by locking homes and automobiles and making oneself less susceptible to personal attacks. No place is idyllic when it comes to living real life on a daily basis, but Fairhope was about as close to the imaginary kingdom of Camelot as anywhere in the state.

Everything previously mentioned about the pretty little city of Fairhope made the gruesome discovery of a man's body in the water hazard on the fairway of the 13th hole even more difficult to grasp. The tee boxes and greens of the Rocky Creek Golf Course were "whipped" each morning to remove the due caused by the high concentration of humidity and fog that were prevalent in the summer and fall months of the year. The first thing someone needs to do before he mows a green is to arrive at the green and whip the dew from the grass. This is to prevent any disease from being moved around the entire green while the water is moved around on the bottom of the mower. It also prevents burn spots appearing where the dew has been forced down into the fine grass by golfers walking on the green when playing out a putt. The groundskeeper would make his inspection of all the greens and tee boxes before he allowed the mowers to be used for the daily cutting. If there were any significant amounts of dew or moisture on the greens, the greenskeeper would have an employee use a dew whipping pole attached to a long rope to run across the surface of the green or tee box to remove an excess of moisture before the mowing could begin. The body of a PGA player, Larry Washington, was found with his head below the water line of the water hazard, with a bloody putter lying by his head. The worker immediately radioed the golf superintendent who was on the scene within minutes to assess the situation.

Gary Tillis, the golf superintendent for the Rocky Creek Golf Course, used his cell phone and placed a 911 call to the EMS of Baldwin County. It appeared that Washington was dead, but Tillis made his call to the EMS as a matter of procedure, and to make sure no possible evidence of the crime would be disturbed by them examining the body. Gary had watched enough crime shows on television to know that a crime scene needed to be preserved intact for the authorities to be able to follow clues and possible evidence left by the killer. Within twenty minutes an EMS vehicle arrived, and two medics hurried over to the body to check Larry Washington for a pulse and other signs of life. It was obvious to Gary that Washington was indeed dead, because the medics put their instruments back into their medical bags and headed back to their vehicle. One of the medics told Gary that he had notified the Fairhope Police Chief, and he also had contacted the coroner's office. He predicted that both the police department and the coroner's van would arrive within the hour. The superintendent called the president of the Rocky Creek Golf Club, and he in turn called his close friend, Mayor Todd Jackson. Todd lived in one of the larger homes on the golf course, and within minutes of his notification from Gary Tillis, he was on the phone to Governor Big Jim Flowers' office.

"Governor, we have a situation down here in Fairhope that goes well beyond our ability to control all the ramifications of the event. My police chief, Colonel Rocky Crawford, has visited the scene of a murder this morning, and the situation is sensitive, to say the least."

"Murder? What happened Mayor?"

"Normally, I would not concern you with our problems in the City of Fairhope, but this is a little unusual, and as I said before, 'sensitive.' I know you're familiar with Larry Washington. Right?"

"The PGA champion of a few years ago? Sure, I know him. Is he in some kind of trouble?"

"No, Sir. He's the person who was murdered."

"Oh, no! What happened?"

"We're not sure at this point, but it appears that he was hit in the back of the head with a gold club, possibly a putter. We found the putter close to the body, on the apron of the 13th green, and we are not sure if there are any other wounds or another cause of death. The coroner is on her way to the scene, and I will try to get her to share what she may know with us before she leaves with the body for an autopsy. As you know, Rocky Creek Golf Course is very important to the health and financial security to the City of Fairhope. We need to hire a private detective agency to help us wrap the investigation as soon as possible so we can begin damage control. Can you recommend anyone or any agency that might be better than another one to assist us in our investigation?"

"I can, Mayor, but they won't come cheap. They are the very best of the best when it comes to crime solving. They just successfully solved the murders that occurred at St. Thomas Catholic Church beginning with a bishop on St. Patrick's Day. Do you want me to refer you to them?"

"Yes, I do. Cost is not a problem, because if this murder has a lasting effect on Rocky Creek's reputation, hiring the agency will be a minor expense compared to the potential loss of revenue from the stigma that could follow such an event."

"I agree," the governor said, rummaging around in his desk drawer for the business card for The Bremen & Whitacre Detective Agency. "Here it is. Contact John Bremen at 205-555-1234, and you can tell him that I recommended that you call. John and his wife have a small, but very effective, investigation business. As I said earlier, they are the best I could recommend to you and the City of Fairhope. Your police chief will need to give John and his team some room to work, but he will cooperate with your local police department and not shut them out of his investigation. He gets many requests for work now, but if you use my name, I am pretty sure that he will help you."

"Thanks, Governor. I owe you!"

"That's the way it should be!" Big Jim Flowers roared with laughter. Mayor Jackson wasn't sure if he was just kidding or putting Todd on notice that the governor might be asking for a return favor in the future. Either way, his city needed the likes of The Bremen & Whitacre Detective Agency's expertise, and they needed it now. He placed the call immediately after hanging up from speaking with Big Jim Flowers.

"Bremen & Whitacre Detective Agency, Julie Anderson speaking. How may I help you?"

"I need to speak with John Bremen, please."

"May I tell him who's calling?"

"Mayor Todd Jackson from the City of Fairhope, Alabama."

"Hold, please," Julie said, and she went back to the front porch and told John about the mayor being on the line for him. John, Daphne, Clara, and Julie had been sitting on the front porch of the Patterson Mansion, slowly rocking in the oversized rocking chairs and observing the arriving students at Ashburn University who were populating the Quadrangle that lay just across the street from their office. Julie handed John the portable telephone, and he placed the call on speaker phone so everyone could hear the complete conversation.

"This is John Bremen. How may I help you?"

"Mr. Bremen, my name is Todd Jackson, and I am mayor of the City of Fairhope, Alabama. Governor Big Jim Fowler recommended that I call you about an incident that has happened in our fair city. He thinks you may be the best person to help us get this matter cleared up."

"Tell me about your situation, and I'll tell you if we think we can be of assistance to you."

"There has been an unfortunate murder at Rocky Creek Golf Club, and that of a prominent PGA player. We can't afford to have this matter get out of control and have the press blow it out of proportion. Yes, it is unfortunate, but because of the current status of our club and its membership, the press would love nothing more than to drag all of our secrets before the masses and embarrass those who are members here."

"I'm not sure why you want us to come to your aid, Mayor. You have a police force and an investigative authority in Fairhope, don't you?"

"We do, but we think having someone from the outside investigate this tragic event might look better in the eyes of the public. I am a member of Rocky Creek, and many members of the city council and other prominent Fairhope citizens are as well, and we don't want any suggestions of impropriety or that we may have tried to cover up something while proceeding with the investigation. Our people will do what they normally do, but we would like your firm to perform an independent investigation of the facts. You would have the services of the City of Fairhope to assist you, if you chose to use them, but you would not answer to the chief of police, the city council, or even to me. You would be totally independent, and your findings would be made known to me alone. At that point, I will decide if we need to pursue any other agencies to enlarge upon your work."

"And why you think we would be the best agency to assist you?"

"To be honest with you, Mr. Bremen, I had heard of your firm before the governor recommended you to us. I'm not looking for a whitewashed story that makes everyone feel warm and fuzzy inside. We need to know the truth, and your reputation far exceeds the limits of your geographical boundaries."

"Would you like us to send you a fee schedule so you will know how much our services may cost the city?"

"No, that's not necessary. The city will not be paying your fee. Two or three of our members at Rocky Creek Golf Club will cover your fees. What we want to know is if this is a conspiracy or an aberration from the norm. Was this incident an act done out of fear and anger, or is there more to it than that? Do we have someone who is trying to undermine the respectability and honor of our membership and club reputation? That's what you will be doing by helping us determine what really happened this morning at Rocky Creek."

"We will require a $250,000 retainer to be held in escrow until we have either solved the case or have determined that we cannot get that done. However, before I can accept your offer, I must tell you that I have you on speaker phone with the majority of our staff detectives. While we are willing to assist you in any way possible, we will only report the truth. No fee, bribe, or consideration of anything else will convince us to alter our findings to you. If we determine that something criminal is happening that may result in more injuries and deaths, we will expect you to report that to your police chief. Otherwise, you and our firm could be implicated in obstruction of justice, assuming these events are ever prosecuted in a court of law. Do you agree with these conditions?"

"I do, with one caveat. Your firm will inform us first before contacting anyone else about your findings, and this investigation is to be considered a privileged conversation between both parties—your firm and us."

"That is acceptable to us. How soon would you like us to begin the investigation?"

"Today would not be too soon," the mayor answered. "Please have someone in your office provide wiring instructions to your bank, and I'll have the money there by the end of the day."

"OK. I'll have Julie, our office administrator, send you our contract for services rendered, and as soon as you accept it, sign it, and return it to this office, we will consider our firm in your employ."

"Thank you, Mr. Bremen, for taking on our case."

"No problem. That's what we do. However, please call me John, my partner and wife Daphne, and our two prominent detectives, Clara and Klahan. We work on a first name basis, and we will call you Todd. Agreed?"

"Yes, that's fine. I look forward to getting the documents to sign and return to you."

"We will fax them to you within that hour. Good day."

Daphne looked at John and shook her head slowly, sipping her glass of wine as she considered their new employer.

"You couldn't give us a few more weeks of peace and quiet?" Daphne asked.

"You heard the man. We were recommended by Big Jim Fowler. What else could I have done? If we turned down a recommendation from the governor's office, we might not get any more referrals from him."

"Yeah, yeah," Daphne said. "You just love crime-solving, don't you?"

"I must admit to that fact, Daphne. You have found my weakness."

"Oh, you have more weaknesses than that, John Bremen! But I will spare you the embarrassment of that conversation in front of our dedicated employees." John began to blush, and everyone else raised their glasses in a toast. Daphne knew how to get to John, and everyone knew it.

Chapter 2

Checking out the Town

One of the first things John and Daphne always did when taking on a case was to indemnify themselves by investigating their employers before they rushed headlong into the fray. That was important because the general public, the very people that The Bremen & Whitacre Detective Agency drew most of their cases from, judged them from what was published about them in the press. It wasn't always fair to do so, but it was the reality of the business. Daphne and John had hired Julie Anderson for her future potential as an investigator, but her current duties were to research backgrounds on every possible suspect or reference to a case that they might be considering.

"Julie, John and I want you to take this list of people and run a thorough background investigation on each of them. We have our usual sources for doing that, as you know, but we also want you to contact a person with the FBI in New Orleans to do an even more thorough investigation that could indicate any misconduct on a national level. His name is Salvador Buchanan, and he is a close, personal friend of Klahan Chu. When you do your search, if you find nothing that sends us a red flag warning, take those names and forward them to Salvador. He will take it from there. If he thinks that there is anything, we need to know about that person he will contact John or Klahan personally. Salvador worked as an assistant to Klahan when Klahan was the FBI Director in Dallas, Texas, a few years ago." Julie acknowledged the instruction and asked for a complete list of names where she should begin her background search.

"Let's start with Larry Washington, Mayor Todd Jackson, golf superintendent Gary Tillis, and finally, Colonel Rocky Crawford, the Fairhope Police Chief. This is not an exhaustive list, but it's a good place to start." Again, Julie nodded her understanding and compliance with Daphne's request. John was standing behind Daphne in the office, and he heard the instruction Daphne had given their newest employee. He motioned Daphne to the front porch where they each sat in a rocker.

"Background investigations are critical to understanding who we are representing, but in my opinion, they are not the sole reason to represent or not represent a client," John said. "Have you thought about what we should do if we discover that one or more of the principals in our investigation is dirty?"

"Yes, I agree with you that such information cannot be the determining factor in our decision to accept a case, but if we know going into an investigation that our clients are hiding something from the very people who are trying to save their sorry butts, then we have a problem. Whether or not it is a problem that we can live with our not is something you and I will have to determine."

"You don't really trust anyone, do you?" John asked with a smile.

"Well, let's see. I trust me all the time and you most of the time. Everyone else is under suspicion all of the time!" Daphne winked at John and returned his smile.

"That's what I love about you, Daphne. You never hold back your honest interpretation of the facts as we know them. I'll tell you what concerns me most right now. The person who has hired us, although he is the mayor of

Fairhope, doesn't represent the City of Fairhope in our investigation."

"I'm not sure I'm following you, John."

"He told us specifically that the City of Fairhope would not be paying us for our services. He boldly said that he and some other influential members of Rocky Creek Golf Club would be paying our fee."

"And that means what?"

"That means that any information we discover that might make Mayor Todd Jackson, or anyone else who may be a member of the Rocky Creek Country Club, a suspect or complicit in the murder of Larry Washington can only be reported to the policing authorities with the approval of our clients. Do you see why that might be a problem for us?" Daphne thought for a moment and then had the answer for them.

"Not a problem, John. You haven't signed the agreement yet, have you? I know I haven't signed it and we both must agree to go forward to make any contract binding."

"No, I've not signed anything. In fact, Mayor Jackson is waiting for us to send him a hard copy of our agreement in writing so he can sign it and have it notarized. Are you thinking what I'm thinking?"

"Yes, I do believe I am. We simply put a disclosure clause into the agreement that while the majority of the information we discover is the property of the clients, any wrongdoing discovered that rises to the level of a felony must be reported to the local governing agencies, and other agencies that might be affected under the discovery rules, and that the client waives any control over that specific information. Otherwise, we don't take the case!"

"Good. We are of one mind. Let's pull Julie off the background work for now and have her type up the agreement, send it over to Mayor Todd Jackson with a courier, and have him wait for a signature on the document. We will also require that the mayor have his signature certified by a notary public as well. Once we have that document in hand, we can press forward."

"Who do you want me to research first?" Julie asked. "Does it really matter?"

"I think we decided to begin with Larry Washington. We'll see where that takes us, and then we'll go from there," John directed her.

"Isn't he the professional golfer who died? Why are we looking into his past?"

"You are correct about him being dead, but there may be some signs in his recent past history that could give us ideas about who might want to harm him. From the immediate interpretation of what happened to Washington on the golf course, I don't see anything that indicates that this was a crime of passion. It appears to me that this was a premeditated murder, and it may have been made to look like someone might have gotten angry at the golfer and beaned him with the putter. However, a putter is usually a piece of metal one inch wide and three inches long. Although it is constructed from copper, stainless steel, or other metal composites, killing someone with one blow of a putter would take some practice. And, according to what we observed on the scene, the golfer was beaned only once with that particular putter."

"Do we know what the C.O.D. is yet?" Daphne asked John.

"Not that I've heard. Have we heard from the mayor or the coroner the approximate T.O.D and C.O.D. of the murder?" John asked Julie.

"No one has called this office to report any findings of that nature. Would you like for me to contact the morgue and have the coroner speak to you?"

"It may be a little early for that," John said. "The murder is less than twenty-four hours old, and she may have not had enough time to perform an autopsy yet. Let's not rush her, because we need her on our side as this investigation goes forward, and I don't want to enrage her in any way by implying that we control the time and date of her autopsies. She'll get to it in good time. In the meantime, let's go forward with the investigation of the victim, the mayor, the police chief, and the groundskeeper. That should keep us busy for the next day or so."

"That's an excellent idea, John," Daphne said. "While Julie is working on the background searches, why don't you and I pay a visit to Rocky Creek Golf Club? We can see first-hand the relevant surrounding facts that may or may not enter into our decision-making process."

"That's a great idea. Why don't you call Clara and have her meet us there within the hour? Tell her if she beats us to the area to take some crime tape and restrict any foot traffic to within fifty feet of the crime scene. Also tell her to wear her uniform that shows her sergeant stripes, and make sure she wears her utility belt, including her sidearm. I want this to appear as official a visit as we can muster."

"OK. Julie, will you please make that call to Clara for us? Tell her that John and I will be along soon, but I have an idea and that we will be making some stops along the way. Am I guessing correctly, John?"

"That you are, my dear."

* * *

John got into the passenger side of Daphne's Crown Vic, and she raced the engine unnecessarily as they left the Patterson Mansion on their way to Fairhope and the Rocky Creek Golf Club. Daphne and John had packed enough clothes and incidentals to allow them a few night's stay at a hotel in Fairhope. Fairhope was approximately three-hundred miles from Ashburn, and a five-hour drive for most people, even using the I-65 corridor and allowing for only a few stops for bathroom breaks. That is assuming one is driving the speed limit of 65 MPH to 70 MPH most of the time.

Daphne's Crown Vic didn't have a visible light bar on top of the car, but their mechanic had installed a flasher cube into the dashboard console to create a flashing effect of their taillights and headlights when activated. He had also installed a speaker that responded to a microphone that was mounted on the dashboard of the car, as well as a very loud siren that make a whooping sound like an ambulance. John had hesitated to have the police equipment installed, but Daphne insisted on it, and she also promised not to abuse its use. According to Alabama State Law, no one could use blue, red, or white flashing lights on a vehicle, with the exception on private property, unless that vehicle was on authorized emergency business. There had been times when Daphne, John, Clara, and Klahan had been deputized by local sheriffs and police departments as an extension of their investigating authority. In those cases, it was perfectly legal to use the flashers and siren, when appropriate. However, this case was not one where the Bremen & Whitacre Detective Agency had been officially granted that privilege. Daphne always pushed the envelope, and when they had been stopped in the past by local police cars and asked to identify themselves and whether they were authorized to use the emergency lights and the siren, it could have become problematic.

Fortunately for John and Daphne, Governor Big Jim Flowers had given all of John's detective's "get out of jail free" cards, showing them as special agents of the Governor of Alabama. John knew that this situation could change if another governor was elected, and he or she did not approve of such a courtesy. Therefore, John was courting a good relationship with the LT Governor, Speaker of the House, and the Director of the AHP—the Alabama Highway Patrol. John calculated that it would be easier to get them on board than to try to change Daphne's driving habits. Her classic 240Z car had a top speed of 160 MPH, and her normal cruising speed was in the 90 MPH range. Daphne had been stopped for speeding more than once since their move to Ashburn, but before the governor's cards were available, Daphne would swoon the officers with her dazzling smile and long tan bare legs that were readily visible from an observation point from the driver's side window. She wasn't above hiking her skirt up to her crotch, if necessary, while she watched the officer approach her car from the rearview mirror. Amazingly, though she had been stopped numerous times for speeding, she had never been issued anything but a "warning" ticket. In a way, it ticked John off that she could, and would, whenever possible, pull that off to evade a ticket. So, he naturally quit telling her to slow down. It was wasted effort and breath.

Daphne had only been on I-65 for about five minutes before she had the big sedan up to 80 MPH. Since it not only resembled a Crown Vic police sedan, it actually was also a factory designated police cruiser, with the supercharged engine and special shock absorbers that had been installed originally on the vehicle. John had secured the car from a police chief friend of theirs, and she drove it like it was official. While John had complete trust in Daphne as an experienced driver, he still made sure he was tightly buckled into his seat with a special safety harness, and he clutched the panic bar that was installed over the passenger door on a regular basis. When they were not engaging traffic in the cities of Birmingham or Montgomery, Daphne increased their speed to 90 MPH, ran the flashers, and stayed in the left passing lane most of the time. They had passed several other police cruisers running radar, but the Crown Vic looked so official that no none had tried to stop them or even slow them down. The trip that normally would consume five or more hours was shortened by over an hour, and they pulled into the City of Fairhope, Alabama, at 2:00 PM. They had been to Fairhope in the past for a vacation, so they knew the location of the municipal building which housed the city hall, public library, and the Fairhope Police Department. Daphne had them sitting in the parking lot by 2:15 PM, so they locked up the car and went inside to find Mayor Todd Jackson.

The lobby of the Fairhope City Hall was a typical municipal government setup, with different department names on placards mounted over each door leading into the separate offices. The City of Fairhope offices had, in years past, been located in various buildings scattered among the 15,000 citizens who called it home. However, in the late 1990s, the city fathers and the people of Fairhope decided that it would be much more efficient if city hall, the public library, the municipal auditorium, and other city departments were centrally located in the heart of Fairhope. They undertook a major task of building a multipurpose municipal complex that would house all the municipal offices, thereby making communications and assisting each other more convenient. The city hall was located on the far end of the complex, with other offices located between it and the Fairhope Public Library, located on the other end of the complex. Modern parking facilities were also constructed so a resident could visit city hall and the library without moving his car. The only other official departments that were not located in the municipal complex were the Fairhope Police Department, the fire department, and the animal control unit. The police department and the fire station required too much parking to be able to be included in the municipal complex, and the noise and constant traffic of those three departments would have disturbed the peace and quiet of city hall, the city courtroom, and the public library. Those three departments were located just a couple of blocks away from the main city complex, and on a nice weather day one could walk the distance between the main offices and the police department in a matter of a few minutes. It wasn't paradise, but it was a well-thought-out project and it worked well for Fairhope. Before leaving Ashburn, John had called Mayor Jackson and alerted him that Daphne and he would be arriving mid-afternoon, and John had hoped the mayor would find time to speak to them. He agreed to the hastily called meeting, and John and Daphne asked the receptionist in the municipal building where they might find the mayor. JoAnn MacArthur was the receptionist for the complex, and she directed them to the mayor's office with ease. Before they left JoAnn's desk, Daphne asked her a question.

"May I call you JoAnn?" Daphne asked the middle-aged woman who had been peering over her reading glasses at John and Daphne's business cards and detective credentials.

"That's what everyone else calls me, so I guess it would be appropriate. Is there some other question you have for me?"

"There is, JoAnn. I understand that the population of Fairhope is about 15,000 people. How many public works people work for the city? If you don't know off-hand, don't worry. I was just curious."

"Well, let's see. Without speaking, JoAnn pulled out a small spiral notebook, counted the names that had been printed on the department information sheets, and answered quickly. "We have thirty-two people who work in various municipal offices, but that doesn't include the library, the police department, or the fire department. There are twelve police personnel, eight paid fireman, and six librarians." JoAnn added the two numbers together that she had jotted down on a lined legal pad and concluded that there were fifty-eight people on the official payroll, but that there were some volunteers in each department that she was not counting.

"Wow! That's not so many city employees to do all the things you must have to do to serve 15,000 permanent residents. I guess that number swells in the summertime when the golf courses and marinas attract vacationers. Am I right?"

"Right you are. We manage quite well, and we don't have much turnover in our staff, so things run pretty smoothly most of the time."

"Thank you, JoAnn, for all your help. Do you need to let the mayor know that we are here for our appointment?"

"No. Just go down to the door that has 'Mayor's Office' over it and his secretary will get him for you." They both thanked JoAnn and headed down the hall. John had been curious why Daphne was questioning JoAnn about the strength of staff employees, and as they walked down the hall toward the mayor's office, he asked her to explain.

"Knowing how many people work within the jurisdiction of the City of Fairhope is important for only one thing, in my opinion."

"What's that?"

"If you look around you, John, you will see that this is a very nice town, with many boutiques for shopping, quaint restaurants for dining, and antique stores and other variety stores for people to spend their money. We know from our earlier visits to this area that most of South Baldwin County is considered a tourist destination in the summertime. Tourists bring in cash, rent hotel rooms, spend big money for fancy restaurants and other services—in other words, it costs money to live and shop in Fairhope. Now, how much income do you think the average city worker brings in each week?"

“I don’t know, but I’m sure we can get Julie to research that for us. Why?”

“We know that there are some yacht clubs in the Fairhope area, and there are also some businesses along the eastern shore of Baldwin County that need to hire more employees in the summer because of the influx of the Snowbirds and vacation tourists. Right?”

“Yes. Go on.”

“You and I are not golfers, so we wouldn’t necessarily consider the Rocky Creek Golf Club as big deal, but I understand that it is one of the best public golf courses in the State of Alabama.”

“You’ve totally lost me, Daphne. Get to the point.”

“The point that I’m making is that most of the municipal employees in Fairhope go to work early in the morning and get off early in the afternoon. That leaves them several hours to facilitate their city paychecks by working at those places of interest that attract Snowbirds and tourists—and maybe even PGA golfers.” John always felt dense when Daphne had to explain her logic to him. She saw the big picture immediately in these situations, but he had to be brought along logically.

“And you think that some of the city employees may be double-dipping at Rocky Creek Golf Club after they get off from their regular jobs?”

“Sure. They probably only make a little more than minimum wage at the city, but they could earn a lot of extra income as a caddy, someone who works on the greens and fairways, and even in the golf maintenance shop. They could simply transfer the same skills that they use daily in their city jobs to a private concern, like Rocky Creek."

"That's an interesting theory, Daphne, but we have no proof of anything like that taking place."

"That's why they give us badges and call us detectives!"

Chapter 3

Meeting with the Mayor

John approached the secretary for Mayor Todd Jackson with his business card in hand. He gave it to her, and she asked the obvious question.

"How may I help you, Mr. Bremen?" Natalie Poole asked. It was obvious from her calm approach and inquisitive eyes that she was a formidable gatekeeper for the mayor.

"John," he replied in a calm voice.

"OK. How may I help you, John?"

"This is my partner, Daphne Whitacre, and we are here to see Mayor Jackson. He is expecting us." Natalie looked on the calendar that she had sitting on her desk, showing all the appointments that the mayor had asked her to make for him, and she didn't see anything that indicated that John was telling the truth.

"When did you make your appointment with Mayor Jackson?" she asked, raising her eyebrows as if she doubted his word.

"He called my office this morning and asked us to come to Fairhope to sit down with him in person. I would normally handle an initial visit with someone like your mayor over the telephone, but he insisted we come in person." Before Natalie could asked another question, Mayor Jackson's private office door opened, and he stepped into the room.

"You two must be John Bremen and Daphne Whitacre," he said.

"That's who we are. Ms. Poole here may think that we are trying to crash your office, so I thought you might want to put her mind at rest."

"Of course," the mayor said nervously. "Natalie, these are two people whom Governor Big Jim Flowers recommended that I speak to as soon as possible. Please ask them what they would like to drink, and we will go into my office." John and Daphne declined any drinks, and the mayor waved them inside his impressive office. For a small town in South Alabama, John was impressed by the decorating and flair that it revealed.

The office walls were constructed of fine mahogany wood, with several built-in bookcases that displayed law books, leather-bound volumes of the classics by Homer, Shakespeare stories by Sir Conan Doyle, and many American novelists, such as William Faulkner, Ernest Hemingway, and many others. John also noticed a small bookcase with what appeared to be paperback novels on the wall behind the mayor's desk. John walked over and read the name of the author: MW Burdette.

"Nice office, Mayor. How are you able to decorate your office so beautifully on a public servant's salary?"

"Oh, no. This is not what you think. I enjoy being the Mayor of Fairhope, and I have run unopposed the last few terms, but the City of Fairhope did not decorate my office. My wife is responsible for the décor and the books." It was obvious from the look on John and Daphne's face that Mayor Jackson had not explained enough details to them about the obvious wealth the mayor's office represented.

"I'm just surprised that you would sink so much money into your work surroundings. Can I assume you or your wife have resources outside of your municipal salary?" The mayor realized that he needed to share more about his past, because it would probably come out in an investigation anyway.

"My wife and I are not from this area of the state," Mayor Jackson began. "We both attended Ashburn University on the undergraduate level, and when I finished my bachelor's degree, I went to law school at The Cumberland School of Law on the campus of Samford University in Birmingham, Alabama. My wife and I married shortly after we graduated from Ashburn University, and I inherited a well-established business from my father when he passed a few years later. Since I was an only child, the resources came to me, and I inadvertently became the owner of several private funeral homes and cemeteries around the Southeast United States. We also own a couple of successful monument companies. I ran them for a while, but I eventually hired someone to handle that part of our estate, and we moved to Fairhope. I'm a big golfer, and I discovered that one of the better golf courses in the State of Alabama had been built here a few years earlier. Are you familiar with Rocky Creek Golf Club?"

"Well, Daphne and I are more race fans than golfers, but we are familiar with Rocky Creek as a tourist attraction."

"The one thing that was not available when we moved to Fairhope was nice housing on the golf course fairways, which disappointed me a lot. I put a group of investors together, and we developed a housing project that would make sure that the zoning and high standards of houses would be required of anyone who wanted to build a home at Rocky Creek. It's turned out to be a great investment, and the homes are very nice. There are approximately 700 homes built on the course fairways, and the average home sells for more than $500,000. There are some homes that are valued at several million dollars. A complementary golf membership comes with the purchase of a home at Rocky Creek."

"I guess you would say that you and your friends have quite an investment in Rocky Creek Golf Club and its success, would you not?" Daphne asked.

"Mr. Bremen, I won't deny the fact that we are interested in keeping the quality of the golf course and its reputation in good order, but that goes for all 700 homeowners at Rocky Creek." Daphne and John could see that Daphne's last direct question to Mayor Jackson hit home.

"Please call me John and my partner, Daphne. We will call you either Mr. Mayor or Todd. Which do you prefer?"

"Either is fine with me. We don't stand on ceremony in Fairhope," he said, chuckling as if it was ridiculous that someone would address him as Mr. Mayor or Mr. Jackson.

"Just what is it that you think our company can do for you, Mayor, that a local investigation company doesn't offer?" This was a loaded question, because John knew that the governor had referred Mayor Jackson to the

Bremen & Whitacre Detective Agency personally. Jackson didn't speak without turning his thoughts over in his mind and making sure his comments would not be misunderstood.

"I know most investigators do a little background research on their potential clients before they become investigators in their behalf. You will find nothing of import in my biography that I have not already told you. The only thing I probably omitted sharing with you is the location where my wife and I lived prior to moving to Fairhope and a quieter way of life. I was on the city council for a while before becoming mayor of a small town in South Central Alabama. You may not be as familiar with that portion of Alabama as you are in the areas north of Birmingham since I understand you grew up in Ashburn and only recently returned to establish your private investigation agency there in your old hometown."

John and Daphne were somewhat impressed that the mayor had done a little research on them as well. That wasn't always a bad thing, because John and Daphne had nothing to hide that would disqualify them for their detective shields or their ability to investigate crimes. However, it did put John on notice that Todd Jackson was nobody's fool.

"Yes, Todd, you are correct. I grew up in Ashburn, went to high school and college there, and joined the U.S. Navy once I graduated from Ashburn University in the spring of 1968. As you are probably aware, the war in Vietnam was raging at that time, and I chose to serve in a capacity more suited to my education, rather than as a ground-pounder in the infantry. Don't get me wrong. I think the U.S. Government's infantry is the best that money can buy, but it just simply was not for me. Once I had served my country and completed my obligation to my military service, something every young man was expected to do back then, I joined the FBI, worked my way up to the position of Director of the Dallas, Texas, office of the FBI, and later retired and moved back to Ashburn. Along the way, I met Ms. Daphne Whitacre, he indicated Daphne's presence with a head motion in her direction, and the rest is history. We now live in Ashburn, Alabama, and we have established our detective agency there. Everything else about me is just cannon-fodder." John smiled as he finished his soliloquy.

"Very thorough and thoughtful explanation of your business creation, John. I really wasn't snooping on you or your lovely partner, or is it wife?"

"Both," Daphne said. "Look, Todd, John and I have both been in law enforcement all of our adult lives. We have gotten down with the dirtiest, nastiest, and more feared enemies of the land in times past. We simply have decided not to do that again unless we are drawn into it beyond our control, and that's why we perform a background investigation on *all* potential clients. Don't mistake our pleasant demeanors as 'non-violent' operators who have no experience in the dark side of crime." John could see that Daphne wanted to pull her Glock and put a round between Mayor Jackson's eyes. He decided to calm the scene by returning to their original purpose of visiting him today.

"Again, Todd, let me ask you why do you think we can make a difference in the investigation of Larry Washington's death? We will do the same things that a local detective agency will perform, albeit maybe with a different approach."

"If Big Jim Flowers says you're the best—you're the best, in my book. My personal company has backed the governor in his political campaigns since he was a local alderman in Eufaula, Alabama. That's where my personal fortune was built, and that's where I was mayor for several terms. Big Jim and I have worked together many years on various projects that have interested us. I trust him as I would a brother."

"Is the governor an investor in Rocky Creek Golf Club?" Daphne asked.

"Let's say he's a 'silent' partner. He has had made some financial investment in the past, he sits on our board of directors, and he owns a home on the 15th fairway. As you can probably guess, he spends most of his time in the Capitol Building on Dexter Avenue in Montgomery, or in his private residence located nearby. He does get away from all that chaos occasionally, and he comes to Fairhope and his vacation home at Rocky Creek whenever he gets the opportunity. Unfortunately for him, that's not very often. He told me one time that he plans to relocate his entire family to Fairhope once he retires from public life. So, yes, he has an interest in Rocky Creek Golf Club, but it's only from an investment point of view, and nothing more."

"Thank you for that information, Todd. Before we can make a full commitment to take you on as a client we need to have as much information that is available about the members of the board of directors for Rocky Creek, and we need a commitment from you that as our client you will not purposely mislead us in our investigation. Although we are not official sworn police officers of any city or county in the State of Alabama, we do work for many of them and we cannot jeopardize our relationship with them by doing anything that's suspect."

"What else?"

"If we discover something that is detrimental to the Rocky Creek Golf Club, we will report it to you directly since you would be our client. If, however, we discover a felony that is taking place or has taken place in the past, we will be obligated to report that to the proper authorities. We will give you the chance to do that yourself, but if you fail to disclose such information, we will have to report it. We do not, and cannot, support anything that is illegal or untoward against the laws of the State of Alabama. If you can agree with these stipulations, we will work for you, pending our background investigations of your key personnel."

"I think I can agree to those terms, John. Will you let me know about your results pertaining to the background searches when they are complete?"

"Only if any information that we discover affects our agreement. We keep all background research results in confidence, in keeping with standard business practices."

"In other words, 'no news, is good news?'" he asked.

"More or less. We don't care if someone on your board of directors is unethical in areas that don't confound the law. We are only concerned with those things that could affect the outcome of our research. Any information that we believe is pertinent to you as our client would be brought to you first. If that information or action is not illegal, it is your decision on how to handle it with your friends, board members, and anyone else we deem to investigate. If, however, someone on your board is involved in deviate behavior, or behavior that indicates a felony has been committed or may be committed, you will be informed first. We prefer not to go to the local constabulary with such a report. Do you understand our position?"

"I read you loud and clear," he said. "Have you decided what your fee will be for these services?"

"Before I share the amount of our fee, let me tell you what we are going to do for you for whatever fee we require. First, we will thoroughly research any person professionally connected with Rocky Creek Golf Club—the manager, greenskeeper, caddies, pro shop operator, serving staff, and even the ball boys, if you employ them. Then, we will look at who might have a motive to murder a PGA player on your links. Is it someone who wants to embarrass you, extort money from you or the club itself, or any other crime that can be connected with such a high visibility death? Finally, we will want to know who else connected with Rocky Creek Golf Club might have a motive to cause embarrassment, loss of investment value, or anything else affecting the property. Although Daphne and I are not golfers, we know what a standing Rocky Creek Golf Club has in the golfing world. I must warn you that the investigation may take us other places than just Fairhope, Alabama."

"I understand. Your fee?"

"We will require a $1,000,000 retainer fee, but we will deposit it in our trust account in your name. As we incur expenses against that retainer, we will happily provide you with an accounting once a week until we have either solved the case or until you decide to withdraw your support. Any funds not used in the actual investigation will be returned to you promptly upon your request and the cancellation of our services. You must understand that we will work independently of your offices, Rocky Creek's offices, and any other board member of the golf club. If those terms are agreeable, I will call our assistant in Ashburn and have her send you our standard agreement. Daphne and I will remain in town until we hear back from you that you have received the document, agreed to its terms, and signed it. Once that happens, we will return to your office, place our signatures on the document as well, and we will be in business."

"When do you think I'll be getting the contract for review?"

"Within the hour," Daphne said, reaching into her massive handbag and drawing out a cell phone. As she dialed the office number in Ashburn, she produced the small notebook where she had written down all the conditions that John had implied to Todd that would be included in the language of their agreement. The phone was picked up on the third ring.

"The Bremen & Whitacre Detective Agency. How may I help you?"

"Julie, this is Daphne."

"Oh, hi. I didn't recognize your number. What do you need from me?"

"John and I have come to a tentative agreement with Mayor Todd Jackson to represent him as investigators in the murder crime at Rocky Creek Golf Club. Look at the inbox to your left, and you should see a draft of our *Agreement of Contract."* Daphne could hear Julie moving things around on her desk until she returned to the line and proclaimed that she had found it.

"OK. Everything on it is complete except for the details I am going to share with you now. I want you to fill in the blanks with the data and information I am going to share with you. Please type it up, print three copies, and FAX one copy to Mayor Todd Jackson to the number I put on a small note attached to the form overnight with the two original copies to us at Fairhope City Hall. Once you have FAXED the document to the mayor, please call me or John and let us know." Daphne gave Julie all the pertinent information that needed to be included in the contract for employment between their firm and the mayor, and she hung up and returned to the mayor's office. John and Todd were talking about deep sea fishing when she walked back into the office. She interrupted the conversation without apology.

"Our office manager will be faxing you a copy of our initial agreement within the next hour. I understand that this office closes at 5:00 PM, and it's now 4:00 PM. If you will wait until it arrives, print off a copy of the document for review overnight, and come to the restaurant at the Fairhope Inn in the morning prepared to sign it, we will be properly contracted to assist you in your search for the killer of Larry Washington. John and I will stay at the Fairhope Inn, and we will see you there in the morning."

"Sure, that works for me. What time shall we meet?"

"How about 9:00 AM?" Daphne asked.

"Nine o'clock is fine with me. See you both then." The mayor offered his hand and both Daphne and John shook it warmly. They left the office and headed for the Crown Vic.

Chapter 4

Initial Background Checks

Julie Anderson was furiously following up on the credit checks, police background checks, FBI verifications, and other security measures that John and Daphne required before they would consent to represent anyone as a client. Since John and Klahan both had been the local directors of the FBI office in Dallas, Texas, they both still had contacts that they could speak to if something odd or unsettling was discovered in any of those basic background investigations. As soon as Todd Jackson had signed the agreement to hire the Bremen & Whitacre Detective Agency to represent him in reference to the Rocky Creek Gold Club activities, Julie got to work getting all the principals of the company checked out.

"Hey, Julie," Daphne said over the phone before she and John sat down to speak to Todd and inquire as to what he currently knew about the happenings at Rocky Creek Golf Club, "what have you found out so far about our new clients?"

"Let's just say that Mr. Jackson's checks shouldn't bounce!"

"That must mean he has a decent net worth, cash flow, and whatever else it takes to be profitable as the mayor of a small town and the C.E.O. of a world-class golf course."

"Net worth is somewhere in the mid-eight-figures, he owes no one any money, has ownership in the Rocky Creek Golf Club, the local bank, two automobile dealerships, and an off-shore oil drilling company. The guy is loaded!"

"It appears that he runs unopposed as Mayor of Fairhope every four years, donates his annual salary to a worthy non-profit organization each term, and has never taken a penny from the good citizens of Baldwin County to represent their interests. Why do you think he wants a job that he doesn't financially profit from?"

"Julie, just because the mayor doesn't take a salary doesn't mean he can't profit from his position as a public servant. The City of Fairhope has a mayor/council form of government, and the mayor has the final say to either agree or veto the commission's actions. It takes an 80% vote of the present council members to override a mayoral veto. From what I understand, Mayor Jackson has *never* had a decision overturned by his council. So, right-of-way legislation, taxes, permits, and other city business has to have his stamp of approval to make it to the construction stage. He has more power than the President of the United States, if you look at check and balances. That's probably why he continues to run for office, and he donates his annual salary because it represents pennies on the dollar for what he can glean from his power as mayor. That would be my guess."

"Yeah, now that you mention it, that's also probably why he is president of the Kiwanis Club, Baldwin County Chamber of Commerce, and the Architectural Oversight Committee for Baldwin County. That's a lot of places where he can wield his influence."

"Did you check for D.U.I. convictions, assaults, or any other dings in Mayor Jackson's past?"

"There is simply nothing there. Either he is a pure as the white sands at the beach at Gulf Shores, or he has paid a lot of money to have his history purged of any wrongdoing. A Boy Scout has a more blemished record than Mayor Jackson!"

"That's good to know. John and I are about to sit down with him and find out what he wants us to do for the City of Fairhope that his own police department can't do. While we are meeting with him, please check out the other members of the board of trustees for the Rocky Creek Golf Club, starting with Colonel Rocky Crawford."

"Do you think the chief of police may be dirty?"

"Let's not leave anything to chance. Just check them out, including all the member's names that the mayor gave us who sit on the board for the Rocky Creek Golf Club. If we find no irregularities, then all the better. You can call and leave a message on my cell phone if I don't pick up. Thanks!"

"You've got it, Boss." Julie hung up and looked over the list of names she needed to investigate. There were only five additional names, other than Mayor Jackson's and the Chief of Police, so she got to work.

John saw Daphne closing her cell phone and walking toward the restaurant, and he joined her as they approached the hostess. They asked for a quiet table in a remote part of the dining room, and they were seated several tables away from any other patron.

The dining room at the Fairhope Inn was quaint and cozy, reflecting the original décor established by the architect E.D. Brann when he built the home for the Beckner family in 1906. Writers the likes of Upton

Sinclair and Sherwood Anderson were often seen frequenting the location, and a fish market was established out of the back of the house from the early 1920s, until Hurricane Frederic devasted the entire Mobile area in 1979. A few years after the reconstruction of the residence, the once home of the Beckner family became the now famous Fairhope Inn. Having been restored to its early opulence, the Fairhope Inn Restaurant had indoor and outdoor seating, a white Victorian design, and was adorned with linen tablecloths and silver flatware. It wasn't the most expensive place to dine in Fairhope, but it was one of the best. As they took their seats at a table on the side porch of the restaurant, Daphne brought John up to date on Julie's report regarding Mayor Jackson.

"As you know, John, I am not in favoring of flattering anyone with whom I have known for less than twenty-four hours, but Julie's report on Todd Jackson was outstanding. If I didn't know better, I would think that he was a saint or running for Man of the Year for Baldwin County!"

"Yeah? How come?"

"He is reliably reelected every four years as mayor, donates his annual salary to a worthy non-profit organization, and is very involved in the local community at a level I've rarely seen."

"I am assuming he is financially clean?"

"Yeah, to the tune of approximately eight digits financially. He is also president of several local community clubs, and volunteers his time at the hospital, when needed. The guy's a saint!"

"Slow down, Daphne. What have we learned when we see something that appears to be too good to be true?"

"It's not as it appears?"

"Exactly. I want to assume Mayor Jackson to be a good citizen and a worthy client, but let's not let our guard down until we get to know him and the City of Fairhope much better."

"You're right, John. Although Julie ran his past through the likes of the F.B.I., the N.S.A., all three credit bureaus, and local police databanks—nothing sent up a red flag. He appears clean."

"Let's go with that assumption until it is proven incorrect. How about the other board members of the Rocky Creek Golf Club?"

"She's working on it. When we gave her the assignment it was near the end of the business day yesterday, and most of the agencies she needed to speak to were either closed or closing. She is working on our list of potential clients right now." Daphne looked at her watch. It was 8:57 AM, and she saw Mayor Jackson, along with a well-dressed man in his late 60s or early 70s speaking to the hostess. She pointed to their table, and they approached with big smiles and open hands to be shaken.

"Good morning, John and Daphne," Mayor Jackson said, reaching his hand forward and anticipating it being taken and shaken by the detectives. John and Daphne responded with a return smile and handshake, and they invited the mayor and his guest to join them at the table.

"It's so good to meet you again in a public setting, and not my office," Jackson said, milking the situation as only a great politician knew how. “By the way, this gentleman,” and he pointed to the well-dressed man to his right, “is Jim Edmond, one of our board members and a very successful Mobile businessman. Jim lives on the grounds of the Rocky Creek Golf Club and plays there often with me and some other members. I brought him along because he may have some insight into our little problem we encountered with the body of the golf pro found between the 13th and 14th fairway. Jim lives just a few yards off the 13th fairway, and he has a vested interest in what we decide to do today.” Jim nodded toward John and Daphne in a show of recognition.

“Jim,” Daphne directed a question to their new acquaintance, “did you see anything that might have some impact on our investigation?”

“Not as such,” he said. “However, that stretch of the fairway has a tapering slope that becomes invisible to the eye if the golfer hits his shot near the rough. The area where Larry Washington was discovered can only be seen from my house, and that is if I am sitting on the back porch paying attention to what’s going on.”

“I appreciate that,” Daphne continued, “but how does that help our investigation if you didn’t see anything at all?” She appeared to be irritated that a local was trying to interject himself into the investigation without good reason. Jim held up a compact disk with nothing written on its face.

“I thought this may be of help in your investigation,” and he handed the disk to Daphne. She took the disk, looked at it curiously, and looked back at Jim and Todd.

"We have security cameras installed on the back of the house, with two of them looking out to the fairway. There is some footage on that disk around the time of the golfer's death, but we didn't have the equipment or expertise to enlarge the image. I was thinking that maybe you could use them to narrow down your search for the killer." Jim had a smug look on his face once he had shared his information with Daphne.

"What did Colonel Crawford think about the cd? Was he able to discern anything from it?" John asked innocently. Jim and Todd looked at each other uneasily.

"He hasn't seen it," Jim said. "We didn't see any need for him to be too worried about solving this crime, especially since we've hired you to do that."

Daphne turned to Jim, looked at him suspiciously, and asked him what he saw that might help them solve the case of the murdered golf pro. He looked like a deer caught in headlights, and he said nothing in reply. John took up the pursuit, albeit with a softer approach than his pretty wife.

"Jim, we often find that someone who is not directly involved in an incident has some information that can help us move our investigation forward. What Daphne is asking is did you see anything specific that might give us a clue as to what happened or whom might have been present when Larry Washington was murdered?" John and Daphne had learned to let a question become a pressure point that has to be answered by the person being interrogated—the first person to speak always loses. Unfortunately, Mayor Jackson had not attended that class in school.

“Jim, can you help us out at all here? I know you are often sitting on your back porch sipping a libation in the afternoon, and it appears that the murder may have happened late in the afternoon, after the course had closed for the day.” Jim suddenly seemed to come alive, thought about Todd’s question, and nodded no.

“I can’t tell you something I didn’t observe,” he said without fanfare. “I’ll give it more thought, but right now I can’t say if I saw anything out of the ordinary or not.” John looked at Daphne, let out an audible sigh, and told Todd and Jim to let them know if they thought of something. Breakfast was coming to a close, and it could not come fast enough for John and Daphne. John pushed away from the table, offered to pay for their breakfast, but Mayor Jackson waved him away.

“You’re here because the board of directors of Rocky Creek Golf Club invited you to help us with this matter that appears to be a murder on our course. The least we can do is pay your expenses. I have instructed the Fairhope Inn management team to forward all your room charges to me personally. Please feel free to enjoy yourself when you’re not working on our case and let us pay for it.”

“That’s really nice of you, Mayor, but we can deal with expenses once we have established that we are definitely pursuing this matter for you. We are still in the discovery portion of our agreement, and as soon as the background checks are finished, we will make the contractual agreement formal.”

“Did the Chief tell you that he wasn’t going to pursue an investigation, or are you just assuming things that may not be the case?”

Todd's face turned a bright crimson red, and he seemed lost for words for a few minutes. Finally, he said, "What we do locally regarding our investigation doesn't really have anything to do with you, in my opinion."

"Todd, I think we need to clear the air before we pursue this case any further. Daphne and I have been peace officers for years, working with both local and federal agencies, and we would have been very upset if someone had withheld material information from us. If Colonel Crawford doesn't want to pursue this type of information, that should be his choice. Otherwise, we could be charged with obstruction of justice."

"That's not going to happen," Todd reassured Daphne and John. "We have our priorities in order, I can reassure you." John stood up, Daphne just naturally followed his lead, and he stated in no uncertain terms that he thought they should meet with Colonel Crawford before their information proceeded. Todd appeared to be uncomfortable that his authority was being questioned, but he complied with John's demand. Todd picked up the phone and made a call.

"Rocky, this is Todd. No, everything is fine, but John Bremen and Daphne Whitacre want to meet with you. Can you come by the Fairhope Inn Restaurant and visit with us for a few minutes?" Todd nodded his head, hung up the phone, and changed the subject.

"Why don't we order some coffee while we wait on the Chief to make his presence?" Todd began some routine small talk to make everyone feel more comfortable. The coffee came rather quickly, they drank it with little chatter between themselves, and then John saw a rather short, compact man in a white uniform approaching the table.

"Rocky, pull up a chair so we can introduce you to a couple of people from the northern part of the state. This is John Bremen and Daphne Whitacre, the investigators that we discussed a week or so ago in your office. They wanted to meet you before they began their investigation in earnest." Everyone shook hands and exchanged business cards.

"Chief Crawford," John began, "Daphne and I have worked as local police officers, with the F.B.I., as well as with federal task forces in the past. We want you to know that we have no intention of stepping on your investigation into this murder, and we will share any information that we acquire with you and your department as it becomes available. The last thing we want to do is obstruct your own investigation."

"I appreciate your concern, Mr. Bremen, and I look forward to working with you and Ms. Whitacre." John believed that the Chief was being sincere in his comments.

"Please call us John and Daphne. We're not too much on formality," John said and smiled.

"Fair enough," Crawford replied. "I'm just Rocky."

"OK, Rocky. Is there anything we need to know at this point?"

"You're welcome to come by the station and read the file we have begun, but I need to warn you that we don't have much to go on yet. To tell you the truth, we were waiting to coordinate with your company before we went too much into detail questioning potential witnesses." John was surprised at the casual approach that this small town police chief was taking toward a possible cold-blooded murder. John thought he knew what was going on, but he couldn't be sure until they spent a little more time with the mayor and Jim Edmond, and then ran everything by Daphne for her input.

"We will keep you in the loop," John said.

"Good enough for me," he said, offering his hand once more to John and Daphne as he left the table. The mayor and Jim Edmond continued to sip their coffee and chat as the police chief walked away from the table and out of the restaurant.

John and Daphne finished their breakfast and told Todd that they would meet him later, either at the Rocky Creek Golf Club or at Fairhope City Hall. John could tell that Todd wasn't happy that the police chief had been brought into the conversation, but anyone who knew John Bremen knew he would not exclude the local authorities or skirt around the issues of the local constabularies.

John and Daphne went back to their room, sat down in two of the comfortable wing chairs that helped form a seating area, and both were silent as they mulled over the conversations that they had just had with Mayor Jackson and Jim Edmond. Daphne, as usual, was the first to speak.

"Did you believe the story that Jim Edmond told us? Why would he come to the meeting if he had nothing to share? I may be a bit paranoid, but that seems very odd to me. A very successful businessman, taking time out of a productive day to meet detectives and having nothing to say to clarify any facts of the case. Doesn't that seem a bit odd to you?" John was staring out of the window at the trees that surrounded the hotel, apparently not listening to her. "Did you hear me?" she asked, somewhat peeved at his inattention to her.

“I’m listening, Daphne. What appears to be going on here is that although Todd Jackson appears to be ‘the big dog’ in this matter, he is possibly dragging a bigger dog in to help his case. In fact, Jim Edmond may be the key person in this investigation, and the mayor could be acting on the behalf of Edmond.”

“I think you’re overanalyzing the situation. I do think Jim Edmond is important to this case, but until we hear back from Julie, we don’t know how influential he may be in the Rocky Creek Golf Club’s operations. Why don’t we call Julie back and see what she learned since we last spoke to her?”

“Good idea,” John said, picking up the receiver in the room and placing a call to their business office in Ashburn. He waited to hear Julie pick up the line before he spoke again.

“Bremen and Whitacre Detective Agency, Julie speaking. How may I help you?”

“Julie, it’s me,” John said.

“I’m sorry, John. I didn’t recognize the telephone number.”

“I’m calling you from our hotel room. Do you have any updates for us on the background investigations of any of the other board members?” He paused let her answer before he spoke again.

“I have three files completed so far. One other file is a little more complex, so I’m still working on it.”

“Really? Which one?”

"A guy named Jim Edmonds. He seems to be a 'mover and a shaker' in that community. I have some information back, but the file isn't up to date yet. I do have three other board member's background files completed. Do you want to hear about them?"

"Absolutely, but as soon as we finish this call, please try to complete the profile on Jim Edmonds. We need that info pronto!"

"Do you think he is a person of interest in the murder of Larry Washington?"

"I wouldn't go that far, but he is an interesting fellow. Just do what you can to follow up on his file. Also, run him through the F.B.I. files as well. We'll get some prints for you to run him through IAFIS as well." IAFIS was the shortened version of the Integrated Automated Fingerprint Identification System. John and Klahan still had connections which they could use to perform background checks on suspected criminals using the fingerprint database. They also could employ the AFIS system that was used by INTERPOL, but that would be more difficult to do. They really had no reason to suspect any foul play from Jim Edmonds, but they would keep their options open. While Julie was filling Daphne in on the background information of the board members she had completed, John slipped out of the room and went back downstairs. As he peered into the dining room, he saw Jim Edmond and Todd Jackson exchanging handshakes, and preparing to leave the table. As soon as they made their exit, John moved stealthily to the table, used a napkin and picked up the drinking glasses of both Todd Jackson and Jim Edmond. Seeing that he had accomplished the task without being spotted by any staff members, John slipped the two glasses into a large envelope he had brought from his room. He made his way back to his room just as Daphne was finishing the phone call with Julie. He slipped into the room, carefully placed the two glasses on the coffee table, and began to smile.

"You look like the cat that ate the cheese," Daphne said. "What gives?"

"Fingerprints of our two illustrious guests. Let's see if we can get them dusted and sent to a lab for verification. I don't know that it will lead us to anything interesting, but fingerprints rarely lie."

"Good idea. I'm assuming you don't want to call Colonel Crawford to make that happen."

"Not on your life!" John laughed. "I still have some contacts over in the Mobile FBI office. We'll courier them over there and see what results he can get for us. By the way, anything interesting on the other three board members that Julie had researched?"

"Not a thing. Just three people with too much money and no place to spend it!"

Chapter 5

The Broken Silence

Klahan had also worked for the FBI in Dallas, Texas, and had been elevated to the position of Station Chief when John had retired and moved back to his hometown of Ashburn, Alabama.

John and Daphne went back to their room and decided to talk about how the procedure should move forward.

"Let's call Julie and see if she has gotten any more background checks completed on the board members of Rocky Creek Golf Club," John said. "I'm beginning to wonder what we've gotten ourselves into down here." He frowned and Daphne knew that was his gesture that screamed "be careful!" After working together for so many years, and now being married for the last few years, Daphne knew John about as well as anyone could know him. He was not a complex man to understand, or so she thought. Now Daphne, that was another situation entirely! When they arrived back in their room, the light on the desk was blinking, indicating that there was a message for them. Daphne picked up the phone and listened to the message. She heard Julie's voice and knew there was information about the background checks available. Rather than listening to any details about the background checks, Daphne called Julie for a first-hand accounting.

"Bremen and Whitacre Detective Agency. This is Julie Anderson. How may I help you?" came the pleasant voice of their young employee.

"Julie, this is Daphne. What else have you discovered about any of the board members of the Rocky Creek Golf Club?"

"Actually, quite a bit. First, Gary Tillis is pretty clean. He had a few brushes with the law when he was in high school and college, but nothing in the last ten years. He appears to be on the board of trustees for the golf club, but it appears that he is a figurehead—simply because he oversees all the operations of the course itself. I don't think he has any money directly invested in the course. He lives in town, not on the perimeter of the golf club, and that says a lot about his financial status." Daphne thought for a moment before asking her next question.

"See if you can get us the answer to the following questions. First, does Gary Tillis have kids? If so, where do they go to school? Does Tillis belong to any other golf courses, sailing clubs, or other private organizations in town. And finally, check out his credit rating. Does he owe a lot of money or is he financially secure? Those answers may help us going forward."

"Got it. I'll get back to you as soon as I have some answers." Julie hung up and began to work on her next task. Before Daphne could get settled again, her cell phone rang. She saw that the caller identification revealed that the call was form Klahan Chu, John's best friend and the best investigator other than themselves. She answered the phone.

"Hey, Klahan. What's up?"

"John called me a short time ago and asked me to coordinate with the F.B.I. office in Mobile regarding some fingerprints. Do you or John have the items that need to be verified for identification?"

"No, John has sent a courier to Mobile with them. They should be there within the hour."

"OK. My guy there is Walter Patterson. He's a good guy and he will shoot straight with you. Just tell him I told you to call. Let me know if I need to follow up."

"Not a problem. Thanks," Daphne said, and hung up the phone.

Daphne told John what Klahan has shared, and they decided to give Walter a little more time to receive the glasses and analyze them. Nothing worked that quickly at an F.B.I. office, so there was no hurry to call the agent back. John appeared to be staring out into space, so Daphne asked the obvious question.

"What are you thinking?"

"Let's see if the hotel can get us a large chalkboard sent to our room. I would like to see all the parts of this drama outlined in a logical format. Will you call down to housekeeping or maintenance and make that happen?"

"Sure. In the meantime, why do you and I take a short stroll around downtown Fairhope. It's a pretty town, and I could stand some fresh air."

"I like the suggestion. I'm ready when you are." Daphne took off her heels, John removed his leather dress shoes, and they both donned tennis shoes. Since they didn't have any immediate need to meet clients for a while, they dressed in casual attire and left their room for the lobby.

The streets of downtown Fairhope had been planned out years earlier in a grid pattern. As the small city grew, the outer portions of the city had deviated from the strict ninety-degree angles in which the original town had begun. However, the Fairhope Inn lay between De La Mare Avenue to the north and Morphy Avenue to the south, and S. Church to the west. John and Daphne walked north to Fairhope Avenue, and turned west and past Knoll Park as they approached The Fairhope Pier. The weather was great, mid 70s, not a cloud in the sky, and a slight wind blowing across the peninsula from the Bay of Mobile which lay to the west of The Fairhope Pier. The distance to the Fairhope Pier was only a few blocks from the Fairhope Inn, and the two detectives walked hand-in-hand as they approached the historic landmark.

"Nice," Daphne said as she reached up and gave John a peck on the cheek.

"What was that for?" he mused.

"Just no reason whatsoever!" she said. "It's just nice to be in a romantic setting without someone trying to kill us!" Daphne had no more gotten that phrase out of her mouth until they heard a couple of rifle shots. They looked around, ducked for cover, and saw a man lying on the pier near the location that they had just vacated. John crawled over to the man, keeping his head down and making as small a target of himself as possible. John placed his finger on the victim's neck and felt a pulse. He was in apparently having a panic attack or something of that nature. John saw that the victim had no bullet holes in his clothing, just dirt and sand from the wharf. John pulled his cell phone out, called 911, and waited for a response. After describing what he and Daphne had observed, John crept back to cover to wait for the authorities to arrive. While the actual response time by the Fairhope police was only a matter of minutes, it seemed like an eternity to Daphne and John as they cowered under an overturned dingy, doing their best to hide from the shooter. They weren't sure exactly whom the shooter was trying to hit, but it didn't matter. Any bullets flying around their area was enough to make them aware of their need for caution.

Three black and white cruisers came into view, their lights illuminating the sky and their sirens loud enough to wake the dead. No one left the relative safety of their squad cars until Colonel Crawford's command vehicle arrived on the scene. Within a matter of minutes everyone was out, scanning the dock area and searching for the shooter. All that was found were some .762 full metal jackets, the same as housed the rounds for the Russian built AK-47 assault rifle. John creeped out from his hiding place and approached Chief Crawford.

"Looking at those cartridges, I would estimate we're looking at an AK-47. What do you think, Chief?"

"Well, we know it's not an M-16 round, because the M-16 fires a 5.56 caliber bullet. The M-16 round is more equivalent to a .223 caliber, whereas the AK-47 is closer to a 30-30 caliber. Both kill without mercy, but the AK-47 has more punch in close quarters. It's a heavier weapon, whereas the M-16 is lighter in weight and more suited for close-quarter fire." Chief Crawford didn't waver in his definition of either weapon, impressing John with his knowledge of combat ordnance. John picked up one of the empty shell casings and nodded his agreement.

"Where did you gain your knowledge of combat weapons, Chief?"

"Saigon, Vietnam—the Tet Offensive of 1968. It was one hell of a night, John. Of course, Charlie was using Chi-Com AK-47s, and they were far inferior to the Russian Kalashnikov versions we see today. However, they would work in all weather conditions, full of sand, dirt, and muddy water. Our M-16s were a far superior weapon, assuming they didn't get wet, get sand in the firing chambers, and so on. The Kalashnikov fired the same ordnance as the M-14, but while we trained with them in boot camp, we carried the M-16 in Southeast Asia due to their lightweight feature and accuracy, when they weren't misfiring! That was one hell of a time, my boy!" Crawford seemed to have that vaçant stare in his eyes as he was remembering his time in Saigon.

"Welcome, home, Chief. I was over there a little after you, and we helped evacuate some of the South Vietnamese before the U.S. Embassy fell to the NVA. I carried a .45 caliber and had no need for a long gun in my deployment. I was behind the lines most of the time, but I had plenty of friends who fought with the M-16. They actually preferred the AK-47 when they could get hold of one. When they were on patrol in the boonies, they used whatever they could lay their hands on. And, you are most correct in saying it was one hell of a time!" Colonel Crawford tipped his brimmed hat to John as they continued to police up the spent casings on the dock area. Daphne had come out of hiding as well, and she helped investigate the area of the shooting with John and Colonel Crawford.

"Whom do you think they were shooting at, Colonel," Daphne asked.

"Maybe you two," he said soberly. "Prior to your visit we've had nothing like this happen in Fairhope for years. Either your visit has stirred up a hornet's nest, or someone simply doesn't like you prying into their affairs. You and John need to watch your backs from now on."

"That brings up a good point, Chief. Who knows we are in town investigating the murder of the golf pro? We didn't tell anyone that we were coming to Fairhope to investigate, so I wonder how that information got out to whomever is trying to kill us?" John let his words settle a little before continuing. "I mean, someone in City Hall or the Rocky Creek Golf Club must have tipped off the shooter, or even worse, hired him to take a shot at us."

"I may be wrong, but I would say those were warning shots. An AK-47 within the range that you two were positioned is usually pretty deadly. Either the target is hit, or some collateral damage occurs. In this case, it was just a lot of noise." The chief reached down and picked up some wadding that was still stuck in one of the empty cartridges.

"Is that wadding from a blank cartridge?" John asked.

"It looks that way to me. I don't see any damage to the wharf or dock area. Do you see any rounds that damaged any of the sailboats or outboards in the slips?" John and Daphne looked around for any evidence of such damage.

"Nope. I don't think everyone would have been so lucky, and with no damage to the facilities, and no wounds on the guy lying on the wharf, I have to agree with you that someone was shooting blanks, with no intention of killing or injuring anyone. This case just gets crazier as we move forward, doesn't it?"

"Chief, something really strange is going on in Fairhope, and whoever is initiating these crimes just make this personal for us," Daphne said. She had that "This is not going to end well," look in her eyes.

"We have our problems, like any other city near the casinos and gambling places. As far as this farcical shooting is concerned, that's a new wrinkle for me, but not something so unusual that we would call in the F.B.I. or anyone else from the outside." Crawford made his statement with a bit of sarcasm.

"Colonel Crawford let me be crystal clear. John and I are not your everyday yahoo detectives that you hire from the Yellow Pages. We are professionals, we have been involved with organized crime over the years, and we have a personal relationship with Big Jim Fowler. If you or anyone in your department is involved in whatever mischief is taking place in Fairhope, we will discover that fact, and you will not be happy with the results." Daphne's stare appeared to look completely through the short man.

"I don't know what you're implying, Ma'am, but you're on the verge of pissing me off. And, assuming you are successful in that attempt, you may find yourself charged with contempt and impeding an investigation. That could land you and your famous husband in my jail!" Crawford's face had turned crimson as he spoke. John stepped between Colonel Crawford and Daphne.

"Chief, why don't we all just cool down a bit. We are all in this boat together, and we all want to find out who is terrorizing the good citizens of Fairhope. Right?" John spoke calmly, but he had an air about him that got the colonel's attention.

"OK, John. But you need to keep your lady bulldog on a leash if you want to get along with me and my department!" The police chief turned his back on them and walked away. John turned to Daphne who was obviously upset and who had become very quiet. That was never a good sign. Daphne Whitacre was a confident, outspoken detective on almost every occasion. When she became quiet and silent, things tended to deteriorate for those whom she directed her anger.

"Daphne, you can't pick a fight with the local constabulary. You know that, and we've operated on that understanding in every small town where we've worked. The very least we can expect from a pissed off local police chief is obstruction in our investigation. I know the man was out of line, but we have to be bigger than him." Daphne looked at John as if he were a stranger.

"That man is dirty, and I'm going to bring him, and everyone in this little town, down if necessary, to solve this crime. Keep me on a leash? Really? You know me, and you know I will not be addressed in such a manner. Colonel Crawford was lucky I didn't pull my Glock and put a round between his beady little eyes!" John realized that Daphne was not going to be consoled at the moment, so he suggested that they go back to the Fairhope Inn, regroup with the shooting attempt in mind, and start again in the afternoon. Surprisingly, Daphne agreed to his suggestion, and they began walking back to their hotel.

Chapter 6

Fingerprints Don't Lie

Daphne and John had been back in their room for a short period of time when the phone rang on the nightstand. The hotel operator told Daphne that she had had a call from Julie Anderson, and that a callback was desired. Daphne thanked the operator, hung up the hotel phone, and used the callback number on her cell phone to ring their office in Ashburn. The phone was answered on the first ring, and Julie sounded excited and began speaking too fast for Daphne to understand.

"Slow down, Julie. What's going on up there?"

"Maybe you should speak to Klahan. He's right here, and he may be able to explain more to you than I can. I suggest you use your speaker so John can listen in on the discussion."

"Right. Klahan, are you there?"

"I'm here, Daphne. John, can you hear me?"

"I'm here as well, Klahan. What's got everyone in the office in an uproar? Did something happen that we should know about?"

"I just got off the telephone with my contact at the F.B.I. in Dallas, Texas, and you will want to hear what he had to say."

"Dallas? I thought you were contacting the local F.B.I. branch in Mobile? Why the change to Dallas?" John wasn't upset that Klahan had gone to the Dallas office for help, but he did want to know why the Mobile office wasn't able to clarify the background checks that he and Daphne had requested.

"The Mobile office comes under the purview of the Dallas office, and they are the ones who referred me to Dallas. It appears that one of your principals in the Rocky Creek Golf Club is on the NSA's 'need to know' list. His file is sealed by the Agency, and no amount of cajoling could loosen up the Dallas agents to tell me anything about him. I thought you might want to know. It could be a red flag warning."

"Sealed? I don't understand their response to a simple background case. How could that compromise that person's current situation? By the way, just whom is it that is so important that I can't research his past?"

"Jim Edmonds is the one person we couldn't dig up any history on. Everyone else checked out just fine. Edmonds—he's a bit of a mystery."

"Tell me what happened when you contacted the Mobile office. Did you send the fingerprints as we discussed?"

"They wouldn't acknowledge anything about Jim Edmonds—even his existence. Strange, but true." Daphne held up her cell phone and indicated that John should call Klahan back because they had a call coming in from the Pentagon.

"The Pentagon?" John asked. "This is really getting weird. Hey, Klahan, I need to call you back. We are being called directly from the Pentagon."

“There’s no need to call back. I just wanted you to know about Jim Edmonds. Julie will send you the background data on everyone else in an email attachment. Good luck with the Pentagon. Better you than me!”

“Thanks, a lot!’ John hung up the phone and turned to Daphne who was on hold for someone whom she did not know. All John heard was that he was a four-star—the highest-ranking military officer in the armed forces. The only person with more power than a full general was POTUS. Daphne’s cell phone squawked, and the voice announced that General Lancaster would be with them momentarily.

“Lancaster?” John asked, and he looked at Daphne to see if she had any idea of whom the general was or what his function might be at the Pentagon. Daphne just shrugged and continue to listen for the voice of General Lancaster. She didn’t have long to wait.

“Please hold for General Lancaster, please,” the voice announced, just before the call was connected to Daphne’s cell. They continue to hold silently, looking at each other with confusion on both their faces. John was thinking: “What the hell is going on?”

“To whom am I speaking?” a gruff, gravelly voice was asking.

“John Bremen and Daphne Whitacre, General. May I ask why you are reaching out to us?” John wasn’t sure if he should take the lead or wait for the four-star to tell him why he had called. Most full generals didn’t have any problem telling anyone that he was in control of the conversation. However, General Lancaster surprised both detectives when he spoke again.

"May I call you John and Daphne?"

"Of course, Sir."

"Just call me Otis. This is not an official call. In fact, this call never took place. Do you get my drift?" The general let some silence remain before the heard John confirm Otis' statement.

"We are investigating a murder in Fairhope, Alabama, General, and we were performing background checks on the board members of the Rocky Creek Golf Club. It appears we may have stumbled onto some sensitive issue with one of the board members. Can you enlighten us on that issue?" John purposely avoided using Jim Edmond's name, and Daphne nodded her approval of John's approach to Otis.

"Let's just say this is a National Security issue, John. I can't elaborate on why that's the case, but I understand that you were a lieutenant in the U.S. Navy before joining the F.B.I. Is that correct?"

"It is correct, Sir."

"And you now own a detective agency with your wife and partner, Daphne Whitacre. Is that also correct?"

"That is correct. What does all that have to do with a simple background check on one of the board members of a local golf club?" John asked. He had inadvertently raised his voice, and the general sensed the tension.

"Did someone try to scare you and your partner away from your investigation today?" John was amazed that this general, officed in the Pentagon almost 1,000 miles away, could have the intelligence report on a shooting in Fairhope that had just occurred less than an hour ago. John wanted to play along to see if he could get the general to slip up and disclose anything that might shed some light on the shooting and Jim Edmond's past.

"It's funny you should ask. According to the local constabulary, someone using blanks and an AK-47 simulated taking shots at us, but we discovered the wadding that is present in blank ammunition, so we knew it wasn't a real threat. Also, there was no collateral damage to any structure or person, which could easily have happened if there had been live .762 caliber rounds flying around on that boat dock. How did you know that happened so quickly?"

"First of all, John, don't assume you're not in any danger just because blank ammo was used this time. Also, the Pentagon has sources around the United States, as well as most places in the free world, that are a pipeline of information to us. I'm not telling you, or the local police force in Fairhope, to forget about solving the murder of that professional golfer. I am telling you to avoid stirring up too much interest in Jim Edmonds. That's all I can tell you at this point. If we determine that you have a need to know more down the road, we will share that information with you. And, as I stated earlier, this call never took place." Just as the general finished his last statement, the phone line went dead. John looked at Daphne and grinned.

"What? Will you please tell me why you are grinning? We just got balled out by the highest-ranking military officer in the U.S. Government and you somehow think it's all a big joke?" Daphne was at a loss at John's reaction to the general's call. John couldn't seem to stop grinning, and that made Daphne even more upset.

"Look, Daphne. What do we know from our past investigations? When we get a call, or a threat, from someone who doesn't want us to pursue our normal line of inquiry is it not usually an indication that we are getting too close for comfort? Just what is the Pentagon hiding, if indeed that was an 'official—unofficial' call from General Otis Lancaster? Maybe we struck a chord, and we have some big shots in Washington quivering in their boots."

"The difference, John, is that the U.S. Government can make us disappear and no one would be the wiser. This is not your 'run-of-the-mill' person hiding behind some illusion. These people have snipers, secret military prisons, and who knows what else. Maybe we should rethink our position with the mayor."

"I'm going to play the 'devil's advocate' with you for a moment. Will you play along?" Daphne appeared to be getting more upset the longer this conversation persisted, but she had been with John for years and was going to let him have his say.

"OK, but if when you're finished with your situational storytelling, I am not convinced we are on the right path I am going to let you know in no uncertain terms!"

"Fair enough. I agree that the NSA, FBI, CIA, and snipers from any one of those agencies could take us out at any time. However, if they had the go ahead to do that, do you think some four-star would be calling, off the record, and trying to reason with us to lighten up on our investigation?"

"I see your point."

"If they wanted to take us out, they would have already done it. That commotion at the boat dock was probably ordered by one of those agencies, and possibly with the knowledge of the Pentagon. You must remember that they know that I have served at a high level in the F.B.I., and I know the limits they will generally take to protect a source, which is possibly what Jim Edmonds is to them. Am I rolling the dice a little? Possibly. However, we have gotten under someone's skin, and that might be a good thing."

"Are you willing to bet our lives on it?"

"Isn't that rather dramatic, Daphne?"

"If I remember clearly, you were in an undercover unit in Vietnam, you worked for years with the F.B.I. trying to root out mobsters and murderers. You know that there are people in this world that don't have a clear moral code of ethics. I just don't want us to overlook the possibility that General Lancaster's warning was believable."

"Don't misinterpret my remarks and actions. I believe the U.S. Government is capable of all things—good and bad. However, there are some things that we can do to insulate ourselves from the kind of action the government might initiate against us."

"Such as?"

"We make it known with the proper authorities and information what we are doing down here, and we make sure the general and his minions get the message that our mysterious demise, under any circumstances, would reflect upon the Pentagon and his people. That should keep them at bay for a while."

"How can we do that?"

"The way I see it is that they want a 'win-win' from all of this. As long as we keep the facts that Jim Edmonds is involved somehow in this investigation out of the news, the government will see that we are making an effort to preserve their secrets that involve Edmonds. They issued a warning—we adjusted our investigation to include provisions to avoid Jim Edmonds."

"What if Edmonds is complicit in the murder of Larry Washington? What then?"

"Let's not cross a bridge that we haven't seen at this time. We'll handle that kind of issue if it arises. What we don't need is to let Jim Edmonds and his baggage slow down our investigation. Maybe we just stumbled onto an undercover operative who has nothing to do with the murder."

"You're too optimistic. If there's a lot of smoke, there must be a fire!"

"I'll keep the fire truck on standby," he smiled. "For now, we go around Edmonds. If we hit a dead end that can only be breached by investigating Jim Edmonds, we will not rule him out. There are more avenues for investigation than just confronting a person who is protected by the U.S. Government. Let's find another way." Daphne reluctantly nodded her approval of John's deviation from their initial approach to the investigation. They always pursued any questionable source in the early stages of a murder investigation, so this was unchartered territory for both of them. Daphne decided to look at the reports that Julie had sent them in her most recent email message. No one else on the board of directors appeared to have a checkered past, and that was good news.

Chapter 7

Boots on the Ground

John Bremen had been a successful U.S. Naval officer during his time in Vietnam, and he had learned a lot of useful things on the job that could not be absorbed by reading a document or dissertation of facts presented by some academic hack. As he once told Klahan, his trusty sidekick who had lived through the violence of the fall of the South Vietnamese government in Saigon, there's nothing like boots on the ground. In every war that the United States had waged since its inception in Philadelphia in the 1800s, boots on the ground were how one finally contained the enemy and seized control of the conquered territory. The Battle of 1812, the Civil War, WWI and WWII all were perfect examples of such a policy. Even in modern times with intelligence generated from satellites spying from 180 miles above the Earth there was no good substitute for having a human being reporting the facts as they occurred in real time. That's what made the wars in the Middle Eastern countries so difficult. Boots on the ground in Afghanistan and Iraq were difficult to achieve. The customs of a crude civilization that still operated as it did in the 8th century A.D. were difficult to permeate without the live soldiers going from house to house, cave to cave, or tunnel to tunnel, reporting back the status of the bombing and other counter actions being applied by U.S. bombers and other war machines. Once the enemy moved his operations underground in caves or tunnels, electronic surveillance was useless. Just like that theatre of war, the investigation of the murder of Larry Washington had to be done in the open where all the facts could come out and be analyzed. Not being able to investigate Jim Edmonds history was a blow against them, but that didn't mean they were defeated. They would simply have to figure out a work around that wouldn't endanger blowing Edmond's cover or putting them in the crosshairs of the Pentagon. John wasn't sure how to make this happen, but he either had to figure a way around Edmond or return the retainer to Todd Jackson and give up on the investigation. Anyone who knew John and Daphne would be betting against them quitting an investigation for *any* reason. The phone in their hotel room rang and Daphne answered it. She was told by the operator that Julie had called once more and requested a return call as soon as possible. She thanked the operator, hung up the hotel phone, and dialed Julie from her cell phone.

"Hey Daphne," the voice came back when the call was answered in their offices in Ashburn. "I have some news that I think may help you. I'm sure you and John were bummed out about the F.B.I. and Pentagon response regarding Jim Edmonds. So, I took another stab at investigating his past with the back door approach."

"Back door?"

"Yeah. I called the Alabama Insurance Agency Certification Office and spoke to a very friendly lady who was happy to help. Her name is Sylvia Haygood, and she is willing to sit down with you in Mobile, assuming you are willing to drive over and see her." Julie gave Daphne Sylvia's phone number and encouraged her to call. As soon as Daphne hung up from Julie, she buzzed Sylvia's phone. The call was answered after the first ring.

"AIAC Office," the voice said routinely when Daphne's call connected. "This is Sylvia Haygood. How may I assist you?"

"Ms. Haygood, this is Daphne Whitacre. My assistant, Julie Anderson told me that she had spoken to you regarding Jim Edmonds and that you might be willing to sit down with me and my partner to discuss what you know about him, assuming we are willing to come to you. Is that correct?"

"Yep, that's right. However, I prefer that we speak 'off the record' and not in my office, if you understand what I'm saying."

"Sure. We are investigation a possible homicide in Baldwin County, and we are staying in Fairhope, just across the bridge from Mobile. Where can we meet to talk?" The response was not immediate, and Daphne asked if they had been disconnected.

"No, I'm still here. I think it might be good to meet for dinner where we can discuss matters in a controlled setting. Can you come tonight?"

"Absolutely. Where might be a good place to meet for dinner?"

"Noja on North Jackson Street would be a good place. They have semi-private booths where we can talk and not be overheard. I know a little about the man about whom you're inquiring, and I don't think we should take a chance of being overheard. It's a little pricy, but the food is great, and the privacy is better!"

"That's fine. What time is good for you, and should we just meet you there?"

"That would be perfect. How about 6:30 PM. They open at 5:30 PM, but I can probably get us seating during the week on this late notice. Give me your cell number and I'll call you back if they can't accommodate us." Daphne gave Sylvia her phone number and Sylvia hung up.

"Who was that?" John asked as he came back into the room from the balcony.

"Julie Anderson is earning an opportunity to make some investigation calls for the agency. She located a person at the certification office for insurance companies in the Mobile area, and we have a dinner date with her at 6:30 PM in Mobile. Her name is Felicity Brown. Why don't we get a shower, drive over there, and hit a few night spots after dinner?"

"Or just come home and enjoy this four-poster bed instead."

"That'll work!" she said, kissing John on the mouth playfully and running into the bathroom to shower and get ready for their dinner date.

"Maybe we can spend a little time in the shower together before we leave for the restaurant?" He had a "bad boy" gleam in his eyes.

"No way, John. We need to get cleaned up, dressed, and over to Mobile in less than two hours."

"Thirty minutes wouldn't delay us too much."

"Thirty minutes might be good for you, but not for me, if you get my drift. Don't worry, I'll still be in the mood when we get home." John sighed and agreed to forgo his pleasure for a while. He just had to ensure that

Daphne didn't drink too much wine at dinner, because she was easily inebriated, and that would spoil his plans. They took turns showering, both dressed up a bit for a nice restaurant setting, and headed for Daphne's Crown Vic.

* * *

Mobile, Alabama, was the second largest city in the State of Alabama, and it offered just about anything a person desired to do in the downtown area. Founded as a French Colonial Colony in 1702. It remained a part of New France for over 60 years and was captured by Spain from Great Britain in 1780. It became a part of the United States in 1813, when it was added to the Mississippi Territory in 1817. However, in December of 1819 it became part of the 22nd state, and left the Union in 1861 as part of the State of Alabama's succession from the United States. Over a span of just 160 years Mobile had been a French settlement, then British, then Spanish, and finally American. Although Conquistadors Diego de Miruelo and Hernando de Soto, both Spanish explorers, traveled through the area of Mobile Bay in the early 1500s, they never laid a claim to it for Spain. Many people in the Mobile area were still misinformed as to whom really settled Mobile, and the answer was the French.

As they drove over the Bayway Bridge, a large bridge that connected Baldwin County to Mobile County with connecting causeways on Interstate 10, the sun was a bright red orb appearing to fall into the Gulf of Mexico far, far away. The wispy clouds that were over the city were beginning to turn a red-orange color, and Daphne thought it would make a nice subject for an oil painting. Mobile Bay was a shallow inlet of the Gulf of Mexico, its mouth formed by the Fort Morgan Peninsula on the eastern side and Dauphine Island, a barrier island, on the west. Unlike the mighty Mississippi River that was one large outlet into the Gulf of Mexico just south of New Orleans, Mobile Bay was fed by multiple rivers, the Dog River, Deer River, and Fowl River, and was the fourth largest estuary in the United States. It was constantly being dredged to remove the silt and sand washed into it by these feeder rivers, or else the barges and large navigable ships would run aground in the shallow water of the bay. As they traveled over the many connecting causeways approaching the Bayway Bridge, the view was magnificent.

"Doesn't that view look nice, John? Maybe we should move down here for a change. The only large body of water near Ashburn is Guntersville Lake on the Tennessee River, and it's almost 100 miles north of us."

"I didn't know you liked the water that much."

"I love the water. I'll bet it would be lovely living here."

"The statistics say otherwise. According to something I was reading as we were deciding whether or not to take on this case, Mobile has 38 crimes per 1000 residents, and that's one of the highest crime rates in America. Even though murder and rape, the most violent of crimes against persons, is only a small percentage of the crime perpetuated in Mobile, it's still much safer in Ashburn than most places in Alabama."

"I guess you're right, but you must admit the view is a killer!"

"Nice play on words." They had just crossed over into Mobile and their street exit off I-10 was just a few exits ahead. They had exited onto Government Boulevard, a spur off I-10, and downtown Mobile loomed up at them as soon as they crossed the Mobile River. Interstate 10 became the George C. Wallace tunnel that provided passage into the Mobile area by delivering traffic through large connecting sections of pipe some forty feet below the Mobile River. The sections of pipe were made in the local shipyards, floated to their desired connecting points, sunk to the bottom of the river, and connected by divers. It was a unique way to build a tunnel, and it helped move traffic on I-10 by avoiding toll roads or other limitations by overwater bridge and toll booths. However, if one was not paying attention as they approached the Mobile River, travelers would be directed through the I-10 tunnel and away from the heart of the city. The Government Boulevard exit was easily missed by those unacquainted with its function to make access to the City of Mobile much easier. Daphne turned right off Government Street, past the historic Admiral Semmes Hotel, and saw the Noja Restaurant on their right. There was valet parking, so Daphne parked and gave the key to the attendant. He looked at the Crown Vic with big eyes. He had never seen a monster car quite like Daphne's.

"Take care with my car," she said coolly to the attendant. "I am very attached to it." He assured her he would park it in a very safe place while they were inside the restaurant. John smiled to himself without Daphne noticing. She treated that Crown Vic better than him at times. As they approached the front door, John saw a very attractive brunette just entering the restaurant before they arrived. She didn't look anything like an F.B.I. agent or employee.

"So, is that pretty young woman Felicity Brown, our possible F.B.I. informant?"

"You think she is a plant by the Company to throw us off?"

"It wouldn't be the first time. And, by the way, just because she's a looker doesn't mean you can flirt with her to get her to spill the beans!"

"I do declare, Daphne, I think you may be jealous."

"Don't push your luck, John. I have a pearl-handled, .38 caliber pistol in my clutch bag. Try and remember that!" Daphne didn't smile when she made the declaration, so John cooled it on the sarcasm. Daphne's red hair was her natural color, and her temperament often matched the fiery color of that hair.

"Right! I'll try to remember that fact." He smiled at his pretty wife, took her arm, and guided her into the restaurant. The pretty young F.B.I. woman was sitting on a small couch waiting to be seated with them. "Felicity?" John asked.

"Yes. You must be John and Daphne," she said, looking over both of them with critical eyes. "I hope I can be of some assistance to you, but there are some things I cannot share. I understand you worked for the F.B.I. at one time, so you'll understand the restrictions." She made her statement with confidence that she wasn't telling John anything that he didn't already know.

"Yes, I do understand. However, Klahan Chu, our investigator who spoke to you earlier, said you might be able to assist us in our investigation regarding Jim Edmonds. Is that correct, or did I misunderstand the details?"

“Well, yes and no,” Felicity replied, further confusing the detectives.

“Which one is it? Yes or no? I’m a little confused by your answer.”

“Let’s get a table and I’ll explain my answer.” The maître d showed them to a discreet table near the rear of the restaurant. It was a completely enclosed booth with no other table nearby. “This table is perfect,” Felicity said to the maître d, gave him a tip, and motioned to John and Daphne to sit first, then she slid into the booth across from them. It was obvious that something was up, but John wasn’t sure how to proceed questioning Felicity Brown. She saved him the trouble of figuring out how to proceed by starting a new line of questioning.

“John, this may seem unusual to you, but let me say that there are forces in the F.B.I. who not only condone what you’re doing in your investigation but want to encourage you as well. In fact, this meeting is off the record, and we will deny any knowledge of our conversation today. Do you understand?” John looked at Daphne who looked back with raised eyebrows, and then responded to Felicity.

“Ms. Brown,” I’ve never looked a gift-horse in the mouth, if you understand that old saying.”

“Oh, yes, John, I understand it well. And, please, call me Felicity.”

“May I ask whom our benefactor with any information about Jim Edmonds is, or is that one of those unanswerable questions?”

“Let me just say that someone who is sworn to secrecy and who took an oath to protect certain information believes you should have the information I am going to share with you and Daphne tonight. I’ll leave it at that.” The waiter came back to the table for their order, and they all chose the filet mignon with seasonal vegetables. After Felicity chose an appropriate red wine to accompany their dinner, the waiter left. She continued with her explanation as to why she was really there.

“John, Mr. Edmonds is a very powerful man, has friends deeply placed in the agency, and we need to proceed with caution. He could make your lives, as well as mine, very uncomfortable. So, if I refuse to answer a specific question, please know that there are limits as to what I may tell you.”

“OK. For starters, was he the reason we were targeted with the attempt to scare us away with fake gunfire on the boat docks?”

“Indirectly, I would say yes. I don’t believe your lives are in danger, but rather the agency just wanted to give you a good scare, as well as get your attention. I doubt that will happen again, but I can’t guarantee it won’t.”

“Understood. Let me see if I understand what you’re trying to tell us. We are getting too close to someone or something that needs to remain secret, hence, the scare at the boat docks? Would you agree that statement sums up our current situation?”

“The agency never wants to air its dirty laundry, and Jim Edmonds is as dirty as can be. However, he has enough money and influence behind him to afford him a blanket of protection, under most circumstances."

"Are you tell me that we need to find another reason to investigate him—maybe corruption or fraudulent activity?" Felicity opened a valise that she had brought into the restaurant with her. She discreetly slipped a sealed manila envelope to John, instructing him to wait until after dinner to open it. She said she didn't want to be in his company when he read the contents—plausible deniability, or something like that. John nodded his head, acknowledging the conditions of receiving whatever lay inside the envelope. Just then their dinner came, they ate and drank wine cordially, and without further explanation Felicity excused herself from the table. She informed them that she had to be somewhere else, that the tab for the dinner and wine had been taken care of, and then she seemed to disappear mysteriously. John and Daphne looked at each other with more questions than answers.

"People like that give me the creeps!" Daphne said. "I'm assuming we will find some help in that envelope. Do we open it here or back at our hotel?"

"I think we better wait until we are in a secure facility, don't you agree? There's a lot of cloak-and-dagger stuff going on with Jim Edmonds. He may be a key to solving the murder of Larry Washington, or this may all be just a smoke screen."

"What reason would the agency have to mislead us?"

"Daphne, Daphne, Daphne," John said with a smirk. "Really? Of all people who should know that answer to your question, you should be the first to come up with a plausible answer. Why do you think the agency might want to misinform or redirect our investigation?"

"John, I hate to think our own government has some clandestine operation underway to mess with our heads or the outcome of our investigation. What basis are you using to assume we may be led astray?"

"Bay of Pigs, Contras, Vietnam—how many more do you want?"

"OK, I agree, they do have a shaky track record, but why would the U.S. Government not want us to solve the murder of a high-visibility sports figure? How can that have National Security implications? I don't understand their approach, assuming it is some kind of coverup."

"Maybe it is, and maybe it isn't. Let's wait until we have viewed the information in the envelope before we drive off that cliff." He patted her on the hand, asked her if she were ready to leave, and they tipped the waiter for the excellent service he had rendered. The parking attendant brought the big black sedan around and opened the passenger door for Daphne. She motioned for John to take the passenger side of the car, and she climbed under the wheel. She peeled out of the parking lot and was accelerating through 40 MPH by the end of the block.

"Daphne, we're only driving a few blocks to the hotel." He looked disapprovingly at her for goosing the Crown Victoria.

"What's your point?"

"I thought we wanted to remain undercover, so to speak. This car screams 'look at me, look at me" already. I don't think we need to advertise our presence any more than necessary."

"John, you know how I drive. I like speed and danger. Get over it!" She directed a big smile at him, letting him know that she wasn't upset with the criticism, but that she was a red-headed, hot-blooded detective who carried a chrome .38 caliber pistol just because she like the way it felt to be prepared for anything. She didn't think he needed more explanation, so she gave him none.

* * *

They arrived back at the Fairhope Inn by 8:30 PM, and Daphne suggested that they take another walk down to the boat docks. John raised one eyebrow but agreed that a nice walk after dinner would help their stomachs settle after a big dinner meal. The weather was perfect, and John had his Glock strapped to a concealed holster on his waist, so he was prepared to face whatever might come their way. He never doubted that Daphne's .38 caliber pistol was loaded and in her clutch purse.

Chapter 8

The Plot Thickens

After returning from dinner with Felicity Brown, John and Daphne just wanted some quiet time in a quiet place. They would examine the envelope that Felicity had given them, but they wanted to take a break from the craziness. Ten o'clock in the evening was pretty quiet anywhere in the small City of Fairhope, and it was exceptionally quiet at the Fairhope Marina. Once they had changed their clothes into more comfortable attire, they had walked the short distance to the marina from the Fairhope Inn and were now sitting on one of the docks, staring off into the Bay of Mobile. The Bay of Mobile separated the Baldwin, where they were now in Fairhope, and Mobile Counties. It wasn't a busy waterway, for the most part, with just a few boats and barges traversing the area in the now thick fog which was draped over the waterway like a shroud over a coffin. John and Daphne thought that they might be headed for a coffin the last time they had come to the Fairhope Marina, with what had sounded like live gunshots echoing in the now peaceful area.

"What a difference twenty-four hours make. Wouldn't you agree?" John asked.

"I agree that's it's quiet now and non-threatening, but I'm still pissed that someone would put so many potential visitors to this marina in danger just to scare us off our case. Even without live rounds, some bad things could have happened with that stunt that Jim Edmonds pulled."

“We don’t know if Jim Edmonds is behind the fake gunfire or if it is someone who has Edmonds’ interests at heart who chose to terrorize the innocent people of Fairhope. We would naturally assume that Edmonds has something to do with the incident, but we cannot lay this at his feet—at least not yet.”

“What other reason would someone have to shoot up a quiet marina in the middle of the morning in Fairhope?” John could see that Daphne was still seething from the event which had driven them away from the docks yesterday like a bunch of rats trying to avoid a sinking ship. It was a bad feeling, and he could identify with her emotions that she was experiencing in the aftermath.

“I don’t have the answer to that question, Daphne, but we will persist and pursue every angle until we have figured things out. It would have been very coincidental if those shots rang out just after our breakfast meeting with Todd Jackson and Jim Edmonds. You and I feel the same way about coincidences—they rarely happen. It also raises a question in my mind whether Mayor Jackson and Jim Edmonds may be colluding to keep Edmonds’ past buried and away from our snooping eyes. And, if that is the case, why is Jackson doing so, and what is he hiding himself?” The tree frogs began to sing, the crickets or katydids were also making such a racket that John and Daphne could barely hear each other.

“Are those katydids, or are they cicadas?” Daphne asked.

“Most likely katydids. Cicadas and katydids sound similar, but cicadas only show up every 13 to 17 years, lay their eggs, and disappear again for a long period of time.

Katydids appear annually in the spring and summer, much like locusts."

"Locusts? Like Biblical grasshoppers?"

"What many people see and identify as grasshoppers are really locusts. All locusts are in the grasshopper family, but all grasshoppers are not locusts."

"Now you're just trying to confuse me. What's the difference in them?"

"Locusts are smaller in size, have more developed wings, and can fly over large areas and for long distances. Grasshoppers basically jump, albeit up to twenty times their length, to propel them on their way. If I were going to sum it up in a sentence, I would say that locusts are grasshoppers that have developed a gregarious characteristic. They reproduce quickly, move in swarms, and literally eat every living plant that they encounter as they move through the landscape. There can be millions of locusts in a swarm, thus accounting for the Biblical accounting of a field being devoured in a matter of minutes by a dark cloud of locusts. That's not hyperbole—it's real, and it still happens today in heavily forested areas of the undeveloped countries with little or no pesticide control."

"Yikes! You're scaring me now," she laughed. "How did you become so familiar with bugs? Is there an entomologist hiding beneath those cool blue eyes?" she teased.

"Nope. However, Southeast Asia is a very densely populated region with vegetation so thick one cannot be seen by satellites or spy planes making a real effort to do so. We would occasionally come across areas in the bush where it appeared that a bulldozer had come into the area and stripped it clean of every leaf, small limb, and all forms of vegetation. At first, we suspected the Khmer Rouge, the Communist Party in Cambodia at the time, but eventually it was determined that locusts were doing their thing. I never saw it happen, but it sounded believable to me."

"I guess that means we have katydids, right?"

"Right. And they are harmless. They're noisy as hell, but not dangerous to man or the landscape."

"Good to know," she smiled. John loved Daphne's smile. She could be difficult in many ways, but she had one killer of a smile. "And you're pretty sure that we are safe to walk around Fairhope once more?"

"I think the fake attack on us yesterday was just giving us notice that we were getting too close to some answers to what's going on down here. What we need to do now is determine if there is a connection between Rocky Creek Golf Club, Jim Edmonds, and the pseudo-attack on us here at the docks yesterday. Hopefully, with the information that Felicity Brown has shared with us, we can make some deeper inroads into whatever is amiss in Fairhope."

"Perhaps it's time to return to the hotel and reacquaint ourselves with a celebration for still being alive," Daphne said.

"Does that mean sex?" John asked unashamedly.

"Absolutely."

* * *

Subtlety was not one of John Bremen's greatest qualities, and he had every intention of holding Daphne to her suggestion that they enjoy each other's company before they turned in for the night. As they walked back along a now familiar path to the Fairhope Inn, John's cell phone vibrated in his pocket. He was about to answer it when Daphne asked him if whomever was looking for them couldn't wait until morning.

"I think we really should see who is trying to contact us," John said, looking at the familiar name that accompanied the incoming call. It was Mayor Todd Jackson. He let the call go to voicemail, placed the incoming message on speaker, and they listened to the mayor's frantic message.

"John. We have another problem. I need for you to come to the Fairhope City Hall when you get this message. Don't call me—just come to the office." The mayor didn't leave his name or any other identifying information, but there was no doubt that Todd Jackson was the caller and that he was very upset about something. John didn't know if he might be upset about finding out that he and Daphne were trying an end run around the mayor with the F.B.I., or if it was something else.

"I guess we need to go by the office and see what Mayor Jackson has for us. It's only a block off our way back to the hotel. Are you up for it, or would you rather I walk you back to the hotel and go by myself?"

"That must be a rhetorical question, Partner. There's no way I'm not going to City Hall with you. We are a team, and I want to know what's going on as well as you. Also, remember that I am not the weaker sex!" Fire darted from her eyes as she made her position clear.

"I never said you were. It's been a rough couple of days, and I wanted you to have the option of not going, assuming you just want to go back to the hotel and rest. It's probably nothing of great importance, but we do need to follow up. He is our client and is paying us handsomely."

"We are both carrying our weapons and we are sober. What else do we need to have with us to see the mayor of a small town?" She smiled her wicked smile once more and John directed them down N. Section Street which intersected Fairhope Avenue just a block beyond the Fairhope Inn. The Fairhope City Hall offices were in the municipal complex that housed the new library, the municipal auditorium, and the offices for the Fairhope Volunteer Fire Department. They arrived at the front door of the administration building and discovered that the door was unlocked. They let themselves into the building and followed the sound of voices and the lights that illumined the occupied offices. They could see the mayor sitting behind his desk, speaking to someone on his phone. When he saw them standing out in the hallway, he indicated for them to come into his office and take a chair in front of his desk. They sat and waited for the mayor to complete his phone call. Todd hung up the phone and had a very strained look on his face.

"What's up, Mayor?" John asked.

"There's been another incident in town that is probably related to your investigation."

"What kind of incident?" Daphne asked.

"Another person has turned up dead at the Rocky Creek Golf Club. All the details are not available to me at this time, but I can say the M.O. is apparently very similar to the murder of Larry Washington."

"How so?"

"One of our more prominent members was found in the locker room this evening by the cleaning staff. The coroner hasn't ruled on the exact C.O.D., but it appears that he was struck with a golf club. The back of his skull was crushed, and the nine iron was deeply imbedded in his brain. Although the C.O.D. hasn't been officially designated murder, it's pretty obvious to me that we have a repeat offender or a copy-cat crime."

"You mentioned the victim was a prominent member of Rocky Creek. Can you share his name with us at this time?" The mayor looked down as if he were contemplating not sharing the name, but he lifted his face and told them that the victim was Jim Edmonds.

"What?" Daphne gasped. "Are you sure?" Of course, once she had blurted out her question, she realized how stupid she must have sounded to the mayor. In a calmer voice she continued to ask questions. "Did the coroner have a T.O.D., or is it too early to know?"

"Time of death falls in a window between 5:30 PM and 6:30 PM. The body has just been moved to the city morgue, and Dr. Juanita Haralson, the Baldwin County Coroner, will be performing an autopsy tomorrow morning, beginning at 9:00 AM. She has expressed that both of you will be welcome to attend the autopsy, assuming you choose to do so. We should have more details after she is finished. Shall I tell her one or both of you are interested in attending the autopsy?"

"Absolutely," Daphne said. "We'll both be in attendance."

"As you probably deduced, Jim Edmonds was a personal friend, and this murder investigation has just become very personal for me. I will be available to answer any questions you may have going forward, so please don't hesitate to call my office." Todd stood up from his desk, offered his hand for them to shake, and summarily dismissed them from his office. It was apparent to Daphne and John that Mayor Jackson was emotionally drained by the untimely death of his friend and golfing buddy. The detectives told Todd that they could see their way out, so they walked out of his office, into the hall, and out toward the exit.

"What do you make of this turn?" Daphne asked.

"I'm not sure, but it is definitely coincidental that someone of interest suddenly becomes a new victim of a mysterious murderer. Since you and I don't believe in coincidences, there has to be a thread to connect Edmonds' murder to Larry Washington's demise. Our task will be finding that thread and getting to the real reason two people were murdered at a recreational facility. Golf shouldn't be so dangerous!"

Daphne and John reached the outside entrance to the city hall complex, and they walked back down N. Section Street until it again intersected with Fairhope Avenue. After turning right on Fairhope Avenue, and then another quick left turn onto Church Street, they arrived at the Fairhope Inn. They decided a nice hot bath in the Jacuzzi tub in their room and a good night's sleep might help them clarify things in the morning. They were both asleep in minutes after leaving the bath. The pretty little town of Fairhope, Alabama, was turning into an ugly experience for both of them.

Chapter 9

The Back Door

John and Daphne were up and ready for the day at 7:00 AM, having showered, gotten dressed, and headed for the Fairhope Inn's breakfast buffet. One of the marquis features of the historic inn was the unlimited breakfast buffet which was served from 7:00 AM until 10:00 AM every morning. Locals would come to the hotel just to enjoy the buffet, so the dining room was always busy in the mornings. Daphne looked over the offerings and was surprised that nothing seemed to be missing in the carbohydrate department. There were fresh buttermilk biscuits, blue berry muffins, pecan pancakes, toasted bagels, and French toast. The protein provided was sausage, bacon, country ham, shrimp, salmon, and flatiron steak. Margaritas, wine coolers, Mimosas, and Bloody Mary concoctions were flowing like the Blakeley River that fed into Mobile Bay. John and Daphne could barely take it all in.

"Wow!" Daphne said. "Have you ever seen so much food as this?"

"Only one other place," he said. "Cruise ships have built their reputations on five scheduled dinners, and 24-hour buffets. However, this would rival even those lavish offerings. Where do we start?"

"I'm starting with a Mimosa. I don't know about you!" Daphne laughed as she motioned the server to their table. She ordered her Mimosa, John stuck with black coffee, and then they got serious. John pulled out the manila envelope that Felicity Brown had given him the night before.

"I think it's time to open this and see what possible lead we've been given, if any."

"I wonder if it makes any difference now that Jim Edmonds is dead?"

"I don't know, but we have to look. Also, I want to be through with breakfast and at the morgue for the autopsy this morning at 9:00 AM. OK?"

"It works for me."

John was pondering their next move as he ate his cinnamon bun and sipped on his black coffee. He and Daphne had had so many difficult cases in the past, so this one should not be one they couldn't solve. What had thrown him this morning was that John had figured Jim Edmonds as being complicit in the murder of Larry Washington. Now, he had to go back to step one and recalculate all his deductions. Could the murder of Jim Edmonds be an attempt to cover up some other crime that he was involved in? It might be hard to decipher the answer to that question now that Jim Edmonds was lying on a cold gurney in the morgue. Frustrating as it was, at least there was some movement in the case. What John had to question was whether Jim Edmonds was a victim or a person complicit in the murder of Larry Washington, now possibly more dangerous dead than alive to the original plot? Fairhope was a small town, with small town gossip circles and tight relationships between longtime residents. Adding to all of that normal relationship stuff, just what did Jim Edmonds represent to the mayor and council? After all, he previously was a spook in his former life. Did his former relationship with undercover agents wind up getting him murdered? Jim Edmond's murder generated more questions than answers.

"Daphne, I have a question for you."

"OK, what might that be?"

"What do you think of Todd Jackson?"

"On what level? As a man, a mayor, or a possible criminal?"

"All of those things. What do we really know about Todd Jackson?"

"Let's see. Wealthy, politically secure, and a major player in a small city with few or no limitations. That's how I would sum things up if you limited me to one sentence."

"How did he get wealthy, reach his political level of influence, and become the mover and shaker in the City of Fairhope? It bothers me that we just don't know anything of substance about our client."

"I know there must be another question there, but I'm not sure what that question might be. However, we still have ways to investigate Todd's background and business dealings. I'm sure Klahan still has some F.B.I. contacts who might be able to work up a file on Todd, assuming they don't already have one. Should we ask Klahan to look into things with Todd?"

"It wouldn't hurt to know more about his possible motivation in all of this. Since we work for Todd, not the City of Fairhope, that puts us in a bind if he decides we are no longer needed in his plans. We would have no recourse but to drop things and go away."

"I think I am registering an interest in this case that goes beyond being paid handsomely for helping solve a mysterious crime on the golf course."

"Just for the record, whether he continues to pay us or not, I want to know what really happened to Larry Washington, why Jim Edmonds was murdered, and what, if any, part Todd Jackson played in their demise. Is it related to national security, a personal vendetta, a professional hit by the mob? That's where I get stumped. It's very frustrating!"

"You know what Sherlock Holmes would tell you at this point of our investigation. *'When you have eliminated the impossible, whatever remains, however improbable, must be the truth?'* It appears to me that we simply have to eliminate the impossible—no problem!" She smiled at her husband, and he couldn't help but return her smile with an innocent kiss on her cheek. Let's give Klahan a call and get him to delve a little deeper into Mayor Jackson's background. He probably can get that done through his Dallas people at the F.B.I., and no one will be the wiser. I'm not sure if Todd Jackson has the New Orleans F.B.I. people on his payroll or not."

"Daphne! Do you think a federal agent could be corrupted for monetary gain?" John asked, tongue-in-cheek.

"Have you ever heard of Daniel Brewster, Frank Boykin, Charles Diggs, William Jefferson, Dan Rostenkowski—need I name more? These people were all either Democrat or Republican legislators, sworn to uphold the U.S. Constitution and defend the country to their own death and detriment. As far as I can determine, a mayor takes a similar oath of office, but his stature or potential to harm the country is far less influential than a federal judge, member of the House of Representatives, or sitting Senator of the United States! So, yes, I think Mayor Todd Jackson could be corrupted by money, power, or both!"

"I was just kidding about thinking our mayor friend was above the law. I know some of the names you mentioned either were found guilty, or pled as such, to RICO violations, too. Racketeering acts get down and dirty with crime syndicates, as well as laundering money for the mob. Jackson may be as clean as the driven snow, but it won't hurt to check him out with a little more scrutiny than just a routine background check."

"I agree. I'll call Klahan." Daphne called the private cell number that she had programmed into her cell phone, and Klahan picked up almost immediately.

"Hey, Daphne. What's up?"

"John and I are wondering if you can use your Dallas F.B.I. contacts and delve a little deeper into the background of Mayor Todd Jackson. We would like to keep the search isolated to the Dallas office, just in case the mayor has an inside person in the New Orleans F.B.I. office. After all, he was a good friend of Jim Edmonds, and we know for a fact that Edmonds was on the federal government payroll in some way for a long stretch of time. Maybe the same can be said for Mayor Jackson. It would be good to know that kind of information. Our situation is tenuous here, to say the least, since we work for the man we think may be dirty. Can you and your people be discreet?"

“Absolutely. Jackson won’t even know we inquired.” Klahan hung up and Daphne shared the conversation she just had with her investigator with John. He nodded his approval, and they turned their attention to something else.

“It’s good that we have Klahan looking into the mayor’s past, but there are probably things we can research locally to give us an indication whether or not Todd is involved in shady operations in and around Fairhope. The trick is to find out as much as we can without our inquiry signaling to the mayor that we might have doubts about his character or integrity. How can we insulate ourselves from him finding out that we are snooping?” Daphne thought for a moment before she spoke.

“Easy enough, if you use a ploy to investigate him. You simply let him know that we are investigating *everyone* who is currently, or who has been involved in the past, with Rocky Creek Golf Club. That way he will expect his name to come up in discussions as well as other people. There should be no surprise.”

“I like the subterfuge, but how do we sell it to him? We don’t want him to be suspicious that we are actually targeting his possible wrongdoings or involvement in either of the recent deaths associated with the club?”

“We use a third person approach. Something like, ‘*We want you to be aware that we have a third-party investigator looking at everyone who has been involved with the Rocky Creek Golf Club in the past few years, so you won’t think we are targeting you or your close allies. If anyone complains to you about the investigation, you can assume they may have something to hide.*’ While all the time, we actually are targeting the mayor and his close friends—he just doesn't need to know it."

"You are one sneaky redhead, Daphne!" John held up his hand for a "high-five" hand-slap. This woman continued to impress him as the years passed—not only in her beauty, but also in her sharp wit. He was glad she was on his side! "Of course, Klahan will be our 'local investigator,' so we will not lose any continuity in the historical data that we continue to compile on Todd Jackson and his cronies."

"Now you have the complete picture. Todd will believe he has some inside knowledge of how we are going to pin these murders on someone other than himself or his fellows. And Todd may very well be innocent of any wrongdoings in the deaths of both Larry Washington and Todd's personal friend, Jim Edmonds. We let Klahan dig as deeply as is necessary to either implicate or clear the mayor in both deaths, and we go from there."

"Great strategy, Daphne. Now, where do we start locally to assist Klahan in his mission?"

"Let's get a list of all of Todd's assets that are listed in his public portfolio. Klahan should be able to compile a list for us, and we can do a little research on our computer before we need to make any telephone calls or talk to anyone in person. If we fail to discover any conflict of interest on the mayor's part, that's well and good. If we find questionable information, we turn it over to Klahan and let him run with it."

"I just had a thought and I want to bounce it off you for your input."

"I'm listening, Partner."

"What if we bring Clara down to Baldwin County, employ her as an undercover investigator, and not inform Todd or anyone associated with the Rocky Creek Golf Club that she is actually one of our investigators. We act as if we have hired her as a local gumshoe to smoke out any hidden agenda in which anyone of Rocky Creek's principal players may be complicit? We can get her some dummy business cards, rent a fake storefront, if necessary, and have her funnel whatever she discovers back to Klahan. He can put it all together and the report will be much more accurate than if we rely solely on Klahan's contacts in the F.B.I. Thoughts?"

"Sounds marvelous. Should I set it up with Clara or will you?"

"Why don't you take care of the details of setting her up, get the office space leased, have some business cards printed, and whatever else needs to be done, and once that is completed, we can approach the mayor with the plan. Before we actually sit down with the mayor, you and I will have a session with Clara to ensure everything looks and works as if she is an outside investigator. The beauty of a plan like this is that the mayor's escrowed expensed for our investigation will pay for the subterfuge."

"Consider it done. I'll get Clara on the phone as soon as we finish this discussion. She can get here in a matter of hours, so while she is on the way, I'll get to FED/EX and have her business cards printed, letterhead to make things look official, and I'll call a local real estate agent and lease a small discreet office for her to operate from. We can lease a bit of office furniture, have a local artist paint the fictitious name of her investigation company on the door, and we'll be set to go. I believe we can get all that done in forty-eight hours, or less."

"In the meantime, we need to lay low and let Klahan do his thing with the F.B.I. Since it's Wednesday, let's shoot for having everything in place by Friday afternoon. Can you get it done by then?"

"Absolutely."

"OK. Make the call to Clara, and then set the plan in motion. We may be able to discover more locally than Klahan can find out from the F.B.I. Either way, we have our bases covered." They both seemed pleased with the joint discussion and decision to use the ploy with their own investigator acting as someone else, so now they just had to dot the I's and cross the T's. Daphne made the call to Clara to set the plan into motion.

"While you get that done, I'm going to head out for the coroner's office. I want to see what the real C.O.D. in Jim Edmond's death was."

Chapter 10

The Autopsy

John was told by the local police chief that the body of Jim Edmonds was going to be autopsied in Bay Minette, Alabama, the county seat of Baldwin County, and the location for the chief coroner's office. Dr. Juanita Haralson was the coroner for Baldwin County, and although there were a couple of other labs where the coroner performed autopsies at times, Bay Minette was her preferred office. She had all her files and equipment in that location, and she didn't particularly like loading her gear into the van and hoofing it to all points of Baldwin County. It was only thirty-four miles from Fairhope to Bay Minette, or a forty-five-minute drive, whereas it was an hour drive to Gulf Shores and the South Alabama beach areas. If she had more than one autopsy to perform in the southern part of the county, she could secure a lab for autopsies in Foley or Gulf Shores. It made little sense to transport multiple corpses to Bay Minette, perform an autopsy, and send the bodies back to South Alabama. This particular autopsy of Jim Edmonds would be done in Bay Minette for two reasons. First, Fairhope was relatively close to Bay Minette. And second, something told her that she had to dot her I's and cross her T's on this autopsy. The rumor mill was reporting that Jim Edmonds was involved in some secret activities that might be of a national security risk. The last thing Juanita wanted was more people looking over her shoulder if the autopsy was less than perfectly performed.

"Hello, this is Dr. Haralson. May I ask who is calling?" she said into the handset on her desk telephone in her office. It was 8:00 AM, and she had a full scheduled today in the Baldwin County Morgue. There had been a suspicious fire over the weekend in Bay Minette, and two teenagers had been burned beyond recognition in the disaster. Juanita was waiting on the dental records from the two possible victims before she could start on their autopsies, but she also had the body of a young woman who apparently died of a heart attack, or something similar, and since the woman was in her twenties, the body needed to be autopsied to verify that the C.O.D. was accurate. Then, there was the body of Jim Edmonds—that was something totally different. The last thing she needed as she was preparing for a difficult day of forensics was to have to waste her time talking to someone who was unnecessary to her daily chores.

"Dr. Haralson, my name is John Bremen. I am a private investigator from Ashburn, Alabama, hired by Mayor Todd Jackson to look into the murder of a professional golfer at the Rocky Creek Golf Club last week in Fairhope. It appears that you have another body from that same area that may be connected with that original case, and I am asking if my partner and I may come to the autopsy of Mr. Jim Edmonds. I understand you plan to perform the autopsy on him today. Is that correct?" There was a pause before Juanita spoke, but no doubt in John's mind that she preferred that he and Daphne *not* be present during her autopsy.

"Mr. Bremen, what I do for the county is not a glamorous thing, nor it is something most people would find interesting to watch. Have you ever witnessed an autopsy before?" Juanita's words were crisp and cool, and she didn't expect the answer John gave her.

"Unfortunately, both my partner and I have witnessed far too many autopsies over the years but getting to the truth in a murder investigation is always a messy and ugly procedure. We both have F.B.I. backgrounds, we have been involved in Mafia takedowns that were anything be a thing of beauty, and blood and guts are pretty common to our investigations. We don't particularly relish seeing a body disemboweled and reassembled with surgical stiches, but that's the price of learning the facts in many murder cases. We are not squeamish, and we promise to be less than a shadow in your presence. We promise not to ask you anything while you're working, and only ask for a summation from you when you've completed your work. We have recommendations from Big Jim Flowers, if you want to see our letters of referrals, and we believe what you find during your autopsy of Jim Edmonds may be important for the preservation of national security." John decided that he had said enough to either secure a spot in the autopsy theatre or not. He would wait to hear the response from Dr. Juanita Haralson before he said anything else. Juanita took a minute to form her answer, and then she was very clear about the parameters in which John and Daphne might view her autopsy on Jim Edmonds.

"Although it is not uncommon for an investigator to want to be present at an autopsy of a felon or a possible suspect in a crime, it is rarer than you might guess. My procedure is to perform the autopsy, speak my findings into a microphone that hangs over the autopsy table, and then organize my thoughts and findings in a written autopsy report that is made available to the specific police jurisdiction once that report has been registered in the Baldwin County Courthouse in the public domain. That procedure is normally acceptable and sufficient in most cases, but if you and your associate want to watch the actual procedure, there's nothing stopping you. I will ask that you do not disturb me as I make my findings and report them on tape. Once the procedure is over I will be available for general questions you might have. By the way, Big Jim Flowers is my favorite politician of all time!"

"Great. We are in Fairhope and plan to head your way as soon as you tell us when to come. I understand it is less than an hour's drive by car from Fairhope to Bay Minette, and my partner has a lead foot, so that will reduce our travel time even more."

"I have four autopsied scheduled today. Two young people, a young woman, and Mr. Edmonds. I will perform the other autopsies first, so if you can arrive by mid-afternoon, say 2:30 PM, you will be able to observe the entire procedure. I don't know if you will discover anything helpful for your investigation of the murder of the golfer or not, but you're welcome to observe."

"Did you perform an autopsy on Larry Washington, the pro golfer, last week?"

"Actually, I did perform that autopsy about a week ago. Really sad about what happened to him. I can make that file available to you as well when you are here later today, assuming you think it may help you in your investigation."

"That would great! We will see you around 2:30 PM. Is there anything we should know about the morgue when we arrive?"

"Only that I have a local police officer as my gatekeeper. I will instruct him to let you in when you arrive. He's a little scary, but he's a good kid." Juanita hung up, and John felt exhilarated that they were going to be able to go to the source for the facts about Jim Edmond's death, as well as Larry Washington. He called Daphne on her cell phone to share the good news with her.

"Hi, John. What's up?"

"I just got off the phone with the coroner for Baldwin County, and I was wondering if you want to ride over to Bay Minette and watch the post-mortem with me? If you're too busy with the details of setting up Clara's fictitious office then I'll let you off the hook. That has to be done ASAP."

"Actually, I found a local real estate broker who is handling all of the details for us to put Clara in Business, so to speak. All we have to do is pay her. I can get away in about thirty minutes, if that's not too late to join you for the ride to Bay Minette."

"Actually, that's perfect. The coroner has four bodies to autopsy today, and she is putting Jim Edmonds last to give us time to get there and observe."

"Is she friendly?"

"She's a coroner, Daphne. She is as happy as death!"

"Oh, pardon me for asking. Did she give you some pushback about us observing?"

"At first, but then she settled down and agreed to let us observe. We can't ask any questions as she is working, but as soon as she completes the autopsy she will allow us to ask anything her examination of the body generated in the way of questions."

“Seems fair enough to me. You mentioned ‘*she*’ when speaking of the coroner. Do we have a female coroner?”

“Yeah, but don’t get the idea that she’s cuddly or warm and fuzzy. She’s a bit prickly on the phone, and I can’t imagine that she will be much more agreeable in person. I really do think we need to observe the autopsy on Jim Edmonds first-hand. I just have an unspoken suspicion that the autopsy may reveal more than what has turned up so far.”

“It works for me. I’ll be there within the hour, and we can head out to Bay Minette. I’ll drive, so we can make up any time we lose by my delay getting there.”

“Swell.”

* * *

The drive from Fairhope to Bay Minette was uneventful, assuming driving thirty miles per hour above the posted speed limit is considered normal. Daphne had always had a lead foot, and she drove every automobile she was privileged to commandeer as if it were her classic 240Z. She and John make the normal forty-five-minute trip in thirty minutes flat. John had bought the agency a Crown Vic sedan a couple of years ago, complete with the police interceptor package, and Daphne made the most of her opportunities to open the big engine up as often as possible. John always buckled up securely before Daphne put the car in motion. She was rarely stopped for speeding, because John had negotiated a special governor’s tag for the Crown Vic, and usually they were just ignored as they sped by traffic at nearly the speed of light! They arrived in Bay

Minette an hour or so before their appointment with the coroner, so they decided to take a stroll through downtown.

"Now this is a pretty little town, isn't it?" Daphne asked innocently as she pulled the Crown Vic into a parking place near the Baldwin County Courthouse.

"Pretty enough, I guess," was John's response. "I'll bet they roll the streets up after dark around here," he laughed.

"Maybe so, but there's always some hidden or secret places to have fun in small towns like Bay Minette. The trick is *finding* them!" They locked up the car, started out on foot for a small diner on the square, and were sipping coffee shortly thereafter.

"You know, although this is the county seat for Baldwin County, there has been an ongoing challenge to move it back to Daphne for many years. Since there are only about 8,000 people in Bay Minette, and over 20,000 people in Daphne, I think it makes sense to move it back to a more central part of the state."

"Move it back? Are you saying the county seat was once in Daphne? If so, why did it get moved to Bay Minette?"

"From what I gather, the Native American Indians have been populating the area around Daphne, Alabama, for more than 9,000 years. However, once Alabama became a state, the powers that be wanted the county seat to be relocated to Bay Minette, so they moved all the files in the middle of the night. That happened back in the 18th century. Evidently there are still hard feelings about the location of the county seat for Baldwin County even until this day."

“Aren’t you just a little fountain of information,” Daphne said as she patted John on the thigh. “I like Daphne for the county seat—probably biased because it is my name!”

“I would never have guessed,” John laughed and was amazed that he still found his wife very attractive and sexy after all their years of friendship and marriage. “What shall we do with ourselves for the next hour while we wait for the coroner to get around to performing the autopsy on Jim Edmonds?”

“Window shop, of course,” Daphne said without missing a beat. She could always window shop. These small towns in South Alabama had some exclusive clothes and other items that were not that easily found in one of the larger cities in the State of Alabama.

“Then, window shopping it is!” John proclaimed to no one in particular. He left more money on the table than their coffee and tip should have been, and they set out on a small trek around the county courthouse square. There were all types of small shops to be enjoyed in Daphne, including a barber shop, beauty parlor, local hardware store, delicatessen, ladies shoe shop, news stand, ice cream parlor, and three or four small restaurants that seemed to be filled with local residents. Everyone seemed to be speaking to each other, and no one seemed to be a stranger to anyone present. It was a nice, welcoming feeling that most small towns offered their local residents. John looked at his watch and realized that they needed to be at the morgue in ten minutes. He asked one of the storeowners if the morgue was close to the square, and the local resident pointed to a rectangular building just off the square and within a five-minute walk from their location. John thanked him, took Daphne in tow, and they headed for the coroner's office. They walked in the door and met the very large young police officer who was the apparent guard that Juanita Haralson had mentioned on the phone earlier in the day. Of course his name was Tiny. Tiny was about 6'6" tall, 300 pounds, and he filled up the door as he asked John and Daphne their business at the morgue.

"We have an appointment with Dr. Haralson at 2:30 PM to observe an autopsy. Will you inform her that we are here?" Tiny looked suspiciously at them, disappeared for a few minutes into the inner offices, and then reappeared with a login sheet.

"Please sign into the building and I will show you to the autopsy lab." John and Daphne signed in, followed Tiny down a long corridor that seemed to lead to nowhere, and finally came to a door that had a sign on it indicating that it led to the laboratory. Tiny indicated for them to enter, and then he closed the door behind them and stayed outside in the corridor.

"Tiny, huh? That guy hasn't seen tiny in a decade or more!" Daphne said. "They grow them big down here, don't they?"

"Maybe he has a metabolic disorder and that's why he's so big."

"Right. Maybe Tiny has an *elbow to mouth* issue that keeps him overweight! Either way, I think Dr. Haralson is safe with him guarding the drawbridge."

"You're definitely correct about that point. Let's see if we can locate the good doctor before I freeze my ears off. It must be below 50 degrees in this room."

“A necessary evil, my friend,” Daphne quipped. These bodies seems to stabilize at temperatures less than 55 degrees, according to what I read before we came today. I expected it to be cold in the building, so I wore my long underwear.”

“You’re kidding. Why didn’t you mention that to me?”

“I didn’t think it was sexy to talk about long underwear made of thermal material. Sorry about that. Maybe you won’t catch a cold.” She pantomimed wiping a tear from one of her eyes, much like a clown at the circus might do. John simply ignored her and began to look for Dr. Haralson. He saw her in her office, apparently writing up a report of some kind. They moved toward the door of her office, and she saw them out of the corner of her eye.

“Come in and have a seat.” There were two rather uncomfortable chairs facing the doctor’s desk and John and Daphne each took one. Juanita didn’t speak again for a few minutes as she completed her written report on the earlier autopsies she had performed that morning. “I was just about to begin the autopsy on Jim Edmonds. Please don one of these aprons and face masks, and you can join me in the examination room.”

John and Daphne dressed according to Juanita’s instructions and entered the examination room where the body of Jim Edmonds was lying on a stainless-steel gurney, face up with a white sheet drawn up over all his body but his face. While it was obvious the man was dead, his corpse didn’t look morose or anything approaching unpleasantness. He just looked like someone, or something had removed all the blood from his body that left him a pale gray in color. Daphne and John had witnessed the bodies of many dead people over the years, but Jim Edmond's corpse looked odd to them.

"Before you get started, Dr. Haralson, could you tell me if the color of Mr. Edmonds' body looks odd to you? I've seen bodies where exsanguination was a major cause of death, but it appears to me that this corpse has had every drop of blood removed in some fashion. Have you ever seen anything like that before?"

"To tell you the truth, Mr. Bremen, I've seen lots of weird things in my time as an embalmer and coroner, but Mr. Edmonds' corpse is a bit unsettling. It almost looks like an embalmer has taken all his fluids out of the body *before* I have performed my autopsy. Let's get started and we'll see what's up with Mr. Edmonds' situation." Juanita made the familiar "Y" cut into the chest and abdomen of Jim Edmonds' body, folding back the layers of fat and skin to make the organs visible for the examination.

"I can't believe what I'm seeing," Juanita said emphatically. "These organs look petrified or something of that nature. There is no liquid content in the chest wall, abdomen, or any other part of the torso." She looked for an obvious needed injection point and found one just below the ribs on the left side of the body. "His body has been robbed of all its blood, mucous membranes, and other fluid content. Since the human body is roughly 90% water and other fluids, what we have left is just a shadow of his organs, muscles, and fat tissue. There is no way I can get an accurate measurement of his organs, nor how he died from what is left of his body. Whoever evacuated all the liquid from his corpse eliminated any chance of determining the true cause of death. This is disturbing."

“Who would have the equipment to do something like what you have suggested?”

“Most hospitals have a morgue or cold storage area in the basement for bodies that can’t be transported immediately to funeral homes or county morgues. Funeral homes have all the equipment to drain a body of essential fluids, creating the opportunity for formaldehyde to be reinjected into the corpse to delay decay and odor until that body can be buried or cremated properly. There are some laboratories in colleges and universities where small animals are put through the same procedures as human bodies, but the equipment wouldn’t be sufficiently capable of applying the same techniques to a grown man or woman. That pretty much leaves the probability that Jim Edmonds’ body was treated in a funeral home or hospital morgue. And I’ll tell you something else that you may not want to hear. It is totally possible that Jim Edmonds was murdered by removing his blood and other fluids. Just looking at his heart and other organs does not reveal that he had a history of heart problems or other organ failures. As I said before, I cannot be conclusive in my findings due to the way he was murdered, but it appears to me that he was murdered by exsanguination, and while I can’t prove that fact, it is pretty obvious that’s what occurred here.” John look at Daphne and just shook his head. What a bizarre murder in an already bizarre case.

“I know you are required to report your findings to the county, stating the C.O.D., T.O.D., and any other outstanding facts that you discover in your autopsies. Can I ask a favor of you in this case?”

“What might that favor entail?”

“I’m not asking you to file a false report, nor am I asking you to lie about what you have discovered in this autopsy. However, is it possible for you to report that the cause of death has not been definitely determined at this time, and that the case will remain open until you are able to pinpoint exactly what happened to Mr. Edmonds? It really wouldn’t be a lie, especially since you are not totally sure what happened at this point. Right?” Juanita didn’t respond immediately but seemed to ponder what John was asking. In reality, she was only guessing that someone used an embalming technique to exsanguinate Jim Edmonds’ body, so it wouldn’t really be a lie to hold back the potential cause of death, especially since she wasn’t 100% sure herself.

“I tell you what I will do, Mr. Bremen. I will not establish a permanent cause of death at this time, but rather state that in the near future we will clarify the C.O.D. of Mr. Edmonds when all the facts are analyzed. That is an honest statement, and I really don’t want to have to reverse myself on a certificate of death, if at all possible.”

“We appreciate your candidness in this matter. We hope we can add to the facts that we know about Jim Edmonds in the very near future. Assuming we discover more about his day-to-day activities, we may be able to help you determine what really happened to him while he was still alive.”

“Is there anything else you need to ask me about his case?”

“No, Doctor. You’ve been a great help. We will keep you in the loop if we discover anything that might help you in your resolution as to Edmonds’ C.O.D.” John shook her hand, and they walked back up the long corridor that led to the entrance of the morgue.

"How do we write up that information for the files?" Daphne asked.

"To be honest, I have no idea."

PART II: A DOMESTIC NIGHTMARE

Chapter 11

A Hidden Agenda

John and Daphne had gone to the autopsy of Jim Edmonds with a secure knowledge that he had been somehow complicit in the death of professional golfer Larry Washington. The murder happened on the very golf course where Jim Edmonds lived, and Jim had had a troublesome history which had been covered up by one of the federal agencies—redaction of the past documents detailing Jim Edmonds activities with the F.B.I., C.I.A., or whichever spook agency he had done work for in the past. After less than an hour watching the attempted autopsy of Edmonds, John and Daphne had more questions than answers to the mystery of who might have killed Larry Washington and why. With Jim Edmonds' historical files sequestered or redacted in such a manner, how could he be tied to anything extraordinary in the pro golfer's murder case? The bigger question was why did someone think muddying the water of Jim Edmonds death would keep John and Daphne from discovering the truth? Everything was swirling around in their heads as they drove back to Fairhope from Bay Minette.

"Daphne, I want you to do something for us," John said.

"OK. What might that be?"

"Get with Klahan and see if he can get someone at the F.B.I. headquarters in Washington to check and see if there are historical occurrences of death by exsanguination that are similar to Jim Edmonds. I want him to check on both mob-related and ritualistic links to such instances.

This almost looks like a devised method of tampering with the dead to disguise the actual C.O.D. of an individual. We know from our experience that the mob has no qualms about doing such things, but there may be an alternative reason for Jim's demise. Religious customs and superstitions can't be ruled out in a case like this. We simply must get to those redacted portions of Jim's work history, or we may never determine what really happened."

"That might be difficult. Even Sherlock Holmes' quote on the impossible falls short when one cannot get to all the facts of a case. How do we eliminate the possible if we don't know what the possible is?"

"No one said this was going to be easy," John said. "We may need to regroup and look at Jim Edmonds through the actions of Mayor Jackson. If we find his deep historical files redacted, then we have a real problem. Let's see what Klahan can dig up."

Daphne called Klahan on her cell phone, filled him in on the details of Jim Edmonds' autopsy, and listened to Klahan's input. She hung up and told John that Klahan would revise his approach into the investigation, with Todd Jackson as the primary source for information. He would get back to them as soon as he had something worthy of their consideration.

"I need to get back to town and make sure Clara has what she needs to set up her faux detective agency. She is clever, and I have no doubt she will help us in the trenches discover much of what Todd Jackson make be up to, but she needs some guidelines to make her work more efficient. Do you want to sit in with me on that visit, or do you have other things you need to be doing?" Daphne knew the answer to this question before she asked it, but she wanted John to know that she was comfortable with his input.

"You and Clara have a great chemistry when it comes to things like this. I'll leave it up to you as to how Clara pursues deep research into the members of the Rocky Creek Golf Club. Just make sure she knows that the mayor is our principal interest there."

"Got it." Nothing else was said as Daphne's Crown Vic ate up the highway as they motored back down Alabama Highway 59 South toward Fairhope. They arrived back at the hotel, and Clara was sitting in the lobby waiting for them when they went to the desk for their room keys.

"Hey, Stranger." Clara said as she hugged Daphne. The two detectives went to the outside café tables and ordered iced tea. A very large live oak tree was casting its shade over the patio, and the cool breeze blowing off the Bay of Mobile was pleasant and fresh.

"I think I could live down here permanently," Clara said. "Having grown up land-locked in Cullman, this area is a refreshing retreat from the concrete, asphalt, and gravel that make up most of the areas of Cullman County."

"It is nice. John and I might one day purchase a vacation home somewhere south of here—maybe along the beach. The breezes in Gulf Shores and Orange Beach are even nicer than these." The desk attendant came to their table and handed Daphne a note. She read it quickly and filled Clara in on the plan.

"It appears that your new office is ready for occupancy. Your business cards will be there when we arrive, and a stenciled name is being painted on your door even as we speak."

"And what is my new name and the name of my organization?"

"You are Lucy Ledbetter, and you represent the Ledbetter Detective Agency, Inc., of Baldwin County. John and I will fill you in on what we have on the case so far, and you will need to coordinate with Klahan to share information on your joint investigation of the Rocky Creek Golf Club membership."

"Is Klahan staying at this quaint hotel as well?"

"No. He can do what he needs to do and remain at home in Ashburn. Someone has to hold down the fort while we are scavenging around here in Baldwin County."

"Does the note detail the address of the office and anything else about my new surroundings?"

"Just that it is a storefront on St. James Street, just around the corner from here. Do you want to walk over and see your new place of business?"

"Let me get checked into the hotel first, and then maybe we can all walk over and see it."

"I'm not sure that's a good idea, Clara. You need to know that Fairhope is a very small place, and I'm not sure we need to be seen together outside of the Fairhope Inn. We intend to sell your service as an 'outside' investigator, and it wouldn't help if someone of importance sees us chumming up together outside of work."

"OK. That makes sense. I'll get my things put into room, and I'll go over and send you some photos back in a text. Who did you get to set all this up, and can you trust them?"

"I hired a local realtor to rent the building, order your business cards, and paint the name of your company on the door. As far as she is concerned, you are the real deal!"

"Give me about twenty minutes to get settled into the room, changed for my cameo appearance, and I'll share what I learn when I check into the office." Clara picked up her keys at the desk and made her way down the hall to her room. Daphne walked to her room and found John lying on the bed, sleeping soundly in all of his clothes. She didn't have the heart to wake him to undress, so she just quietly pulled the door closed to the bedroom, and she put on more casual clothes than what she had been wearing to the autopsy. She was going to walk down to St. James Street and see the office for herself, but she was not going to wait and walk with Clara.

When he awoke, Daphne told John about her plans to "observe" the happenings at Clara's new office space. He thought it was a good idea for Daphne to see how Clara was received by the local real estate agent. There was a small coffee shop strategically located across the street from Clara's new office, and Daphne was positioned with her back to the wall and facing the windows that overlooked the street. She could see the signage that had been recently painted on the window and the glass door detailing that this was the Lucy Ledbetter Investigation Agency. She could also see the realtor she had contacted earlier in the day getting the office ready for Clara's visit. Within a few minutes Daphne saw Clara approaching the office, dressed in a conservative suit, looking the part of a local investigator. Daphne was impressed that Clara was able to assume the identity of someone totally unknown to her eight hours earlier in the day. She couldn't hear the discussion between the realtor and Clara, but she assumed it was innocuous and harmless. Daphne also saw Clara give the realtor a check for her services, after which the agent left the office. Clara's telephone rang, and she saw it was Daphne calling in.

"How did things go?" Daphne asked.

"Fine. The agent has no idea I'm a big phony!" Clara laughed.

"Let's hope we can fake out Mayor Jackson as easily. He will have someone check you out, but John and I have planted some fictious information about the Lucy Ledbetter Agency on the Internet, just in case Todd or his minions research your background. We had Julie Anderson create a profile for you on Facebook, Instagram, and Twitter. Anyone trying to disprove your credibility will have to look pretty hard to find out you're not really whom you appear to be."

"That's a relief. I'm not carrying my piece right now, but do you think I should remain armed?"

"Absolutely! You should wear clothing that makes you appear to be a professional investigator, but make sure you're able to carry your firearm concealed on your person. I know this is not your usual profile, but it's very important that Todd Jackson believes that you are truly a local entity. John and I are not sure how he is connected with the two murders relating to the Rocky Creek Golf Club, but he appears to be too close to things not to be connected. What we do know at this time is that Jim Edmonds had a deep cover assignment in the past for the F.B.I. and/or the C.I.A. We suspect that Todd Jackson may be associated with the same people or project that wound up probably getting Jim Edmonds murdered. If Todd is as connected to things as Jim Edmonds, you could be in danger at all times. Since you didn't volunteer for this assignment, we can alter our approach if you feel uncomfortable at any time." Daphne heard Clara laugh at the precaution that was offered.

"Daphne, I've been associated with undercover work for more than twenty years, and it is always a dangerous assignment. If the party being observed secretly discovers the ruse, one is always susceptible to bad things happening. Just console yourself in the fact that I've been here before, and this is not a new thing to me. I like catching creeps anyway possible. If Todd Jackson is a creep, let's nail his butt to the wall!"

"Spoke like a veteran of many years of police work!" Daphne laughed. "I just thought it was fair to let you know that this could be a dangerous mission."

"I appreciate you sharing that information with me, but every day I put on a uniform, and now every day I dress in street clothes for the agency, I realize that I need to be aware someone may be gunning for me. That's part of the job, and I accepted those terms back when I was a deputy with the Cullman County Police Department." Clara walked to the large window in her new office, spotted Daphne across the street at the coffee shop, and gave her a "thumbs-up" signal before she hung up the phone. Daphne returned the gesture, and she felt much better about Clara's awareness that this was a big-time investigation where danger and possible rewards were present. Like Clara said, all of this was part of the job. Clara hung up the phone and began to organize her new office to look like a legitimate investigation agency. Daphne dialed John's cell number. When he answered he asked the obvious question.

"Hey Daphne. Did you and Clara get the office front set up to get Clara established as a local detective agency?"

"Yep. We have her in an office just around the corner from the hotel. The Lucy Ledbetter Investigation Agency—how does that sound?"

"I like it. Lucy Ledbetter? The last name I would have attributed to our tough ex-cop sergeant would have been Lucy!" John couldn't restrain his laughter at the name, and Daphne joined him in his amusement.

"Clara didn't seem to have a problem with the name. Maybe she always wanted to be a 'Lucy' sometime in her past. Anyway, the name is plastered on the door and window of the small office, she has letterhead and business cards proclaiming her new identity, and Julie was able to create Facebook, Instagram, and Twitter accounts to prove her identity, should anyone check on her past. Anyone inquiring about Lucy will be directed to Julie's desk for confirmation through a blind email link."

"Good work! Is she in the office now?"

"She is, and her new phone number is 251-555-1621. Her cell phone is the same, and she is aware that she needs to be cautious when answering her mobile phone if she does not recognize the caller. It takes longer to set up a dummy cell phone, so we decided to use her current office issued number. You can give her office a try and see how she answers. I haven't warned her that you might test the system."

“Great idea. I’ll give her a call and formally hire her to help us investigate the local Rocky Creek Golf Club members’ backgrounds.” John hung up and called the number for the Lucy Ledbetter Investigation Agency.

“Ledbetter Investigations, Lucy here,” was the reply from Clara as she pick up the handset and spoke into the phone.

“Lucy. This is John Bremen of the Bremen and Whitacre Detective Agency in Ashburn, Alabama. We may need your assistance in running some background investigations in your South Alabama area. Will you be able to help us?”

“Probably, Mr. Bremen. What do you need?”

“I will send you a list of people we want you to investigate if you will give me your email address.” Clara looked at her new business cards and saw that she had a new email address assigned to her new office.

“Just use lucy@lucyledbetterinvestigations.com. I will get back with you about my requirements to get started. My agency will be happy to provide any assistance we can for you and your staff.” With that comment, Lucy cordially thanked John for calling, hung up the phone, and smiled. This was going to be fun!

John called Daphne and reported the successful contact with the Lucy Ledbetter Investigation Agency. They both had a good chuckle at the subterfuge, and Daphne told John that she would be back at the hotel shortly. She was still in the coffee house across the square from Clara’s new fake office. Daphne headed out for the hotel, and she was getting hungry for a good seafood dinner in Fairhope. She arrived at the Fairhope Inn in a matter of minutes, went to their room, and plopped down on the four-poster bed.

"Do you want to eat or play?" John asked. "I'm up for either or both!"

"Let's eat, then play," Daphne said. She had the twinkle in her eye that always slayed him. How could he say no?

Chapter 12

Setting the Trap

Having had years of experience luring unsuspecting bad guys into a trap, John and Daphne were in the process of discussing just how they would test Mayor Jackson to either prove him complicit in the murder of golfer Larry Washington and/or Jim Edmonds. The mayor was no dummy, and he was well established in his community of Fairhope. John and Daphne had a common belief that they had learned from reading Ralph Waldo Emerson: "*When you strike at a king, you must kill him.*" To do otherwise could mean your own demise, and the mayor of Fairhope had the power to totally disable any investigation of his possible wrongdoing going forward. Sitting in the Camellia Café, just a short walk from the Fairhope Inn, John and Daphne were working through possible scenarios to make the Lucy Ledbetter Investigations Agency work for them.

"How are we going to sell Mayor Jackson on Clara's agency for help in background investigations?" Daphne asked. "It may seem too convenient for us to suggest her exclusively as an investigator. We should probably look into some other companies as well—maybe an agency or two that Todd Jackson might be familiar with."

"That makes sense. What could it hurt? The worst that can happen is good for us. They uncover something Clara or Klahan fails to find. It appears to be a win-win."

"Exactly. That's a task that should be handled from our home office, and we can coach Julie on how to make that happen. I will give Julie a call after dinner and get her started on it." John nodded his approval of their next move, and they both began to pay attention to the menu as the waiter came to their table.

"May I suggest one of our dinner specials for you?" the well-mannered young man asked.

"We're listening with anticipation," Daphne smiled warmly at him. The choices were fresh locally caught grouper, pan-fried and stuffed with shrimp and crab; locally caught flounder sauteed in garlic butter with capers and hollandaise sauce; and finally, Steak Diane, served with locally grown and grilled vegetables in extra virgin olive oil.

"Such choices," John said happily. "I'll have the grouper. How about you Daphne?"

"I'm going to have the flounder. John will you order the wine?" John nodded, looked at the waiter, and asked what he suggested with fish.

"Any good white wine would be acceptable, but I suggest Pouilly Fume 1998. We just happen to have a few bottles in our wine cellar. How does that sound?"

"Perfect," Daphne replied. "Please bring the wine now, and we'll be enjoying it while the dinner is prepared." The waiter nodded, bowed courteously, and disappeared from their table.

"Fancy!" Daphne said as she placed her hand gently on top of John's. "This could be a memorable night for us." John's interest was peaked at Daphne's statement, and he pursued her comment.

“Memorable? How?”

“Come on, John. Don’t be dense!” Daphne gave him one of her most devilish smiles, and John actually began to blush. Dinner was perfect, the walk back to the Fairhope Inn was uneventful, and as they were preparing to walk from the street into the inn a short rang out. John felt a hot sting on his left side, but nothing more as he fell unconscious to the payment. Daphne pulled her Glock, looked around in all directions, but she only saw the dimly lit streets which they had just traversed to get back to their hotel. Daphne felt for a pulse, found it weak but steady, and called 911. In less than three minutes there were police cars, a fire truck, and an ambulance loading John into the rear compartment for a short trip to Thomas Hospital. He was in surgery within twenty minutes of the shooting, with a through-and-through wound in his side. After an hour of touch-and-go surgery, the surgeon came out and told Daphne that although John had lost a lot of blood, he would be just fine after a few days rest. John was moved to a private room where Daphne took up guard duty until he was capable of protecting himself. Two hours after surgery John woke up in the hospital bed remembering nothing but the walk back to the hotel from the restaurant.

“Where am I, and what happened?” John asked. He was slurring his words some, but that was expected after having been given anesthesia for the surgery. Daphne seemed calm to John, so he imagined that everything must be well, even though he couldn’t remember how he wound up in the hospital.

“Good to have you back,” Daphne said, and she gave John a light kiss on his forehead. “I was getting worried about you." She knew she was going to have to explain things to him, and she didn't know where to start.

"It appears that you and I have made some enemies in Fairhope these past few days. Colonel Crawford is looking into the incident which put you in the hospital, but I'm not too confident in his or his department's efficiency in determining exactly what transpired."

"I have a pain in my side. Should I assume that I was shot for some reason, and how serious was it?"

"Yes, you were shot, but not fatally!" Daphne's eyes teared up as she offered John a smile. "The surgeon said you would be fine after a few days rest. I'm arranging a private ambulance to take you home to Ashburn so you can recuperate without any chance of a reoccurring attempt on your life."

"I can't go home and leave you here on your own," he insisted.

"I'm not on my own. I have Clara, who may be the best pistol shot in the State of Alabama, and I have encouraged Klahan to do his continuing background search from the hotel in Fairhope. He, Clara, and I make a pretty good team. You need to rest. I've spoken to Julie Anderson, and she has contracted with a private nursing service to look in on you twice a day until you are back to work. The surgeon said that if you tried to do too much too soon that you might tear the stitches that he used to sew you up inside, and you could hemorrhage and die. We can't have that! You will go home and do as Julie and the nurse says. OK?" John closed his eyes, nodded in the affirmative, and nodded off to sleep. Daphne bent over and kissed his head gently, then moved outside the room to speak to Clara and Klahan.

"How's the old man doing?" Klahan asked. Klahan and John had met in Saigon, Vietnam, in 1970, and they had become best friends. John had helped Klahan escape Saigon into Thailand in 1975 just prior to the overrun of the U.S. Embassy in what was now known as Ho Chi Minh City. Taking Klahan under his wing and encouraging him to join in the quest for those trying to harm the United States, John brought Klahan to the F.B.I., and eventually to his and Daphne's investigative business in Ashburn. Klahan would give up his life gladly for his friend, and John would do the same.

"He's still groggy from the anesthesia, but he's going to be OK. I have arranged for a private ambulance to take John home to Ashburn while you, Clara, and I figure out this mess down here. Julie has found a nurse to look in on John until he is stronger."

"Do you actually think John will follow your instructions and go home?" Clara asked. "If my memory serves me well, John is a bit stubborn." All three of them smiled and nodded their heads.

"This time John doesn't have the option to stay or leave. The doctor has instructed him that if he damages the internal stitches from the surgery John could hemorrhage and die. That got his attention. He seemed to accept his fate of returning home and running ops from Ashburn. He can be very helpful coordinating things for us, so he won't be useless in his own mind. John is stubborn, but he's not stupid!"

"Good to know," Klahan smiled. He had seen John wounded several times, in life-or-death situations too many times to count, and he had never seen John pull back and rest. Maybe John was getting smarter in his old age.

"How do we adjust our plans going forward with the investigation of Mayor Jackson and the Rocky Hill Golf Club? Should we take our losses and consider that we've done all we can at this point. Klahan and I will follow your lead."

"Clara, that's exactly what the perp who shot John would like us to do. We will do the opposite. I'm not sure how we got compromised in all of this, but the only three people any of us can trust are ourselves." She looked at them for their approval and they nodded in agreement. "As far as I can deduce at this time, no one knows that you are a plant, and no one knows about Klahan at all. He can operate under the radar and continue to search for clues as to the goodness or failings of Mayor Jackson. You, on the other hand, are out in the open as Lucy Ledbetter. I cannot tell you that your life is not in danger, because it could be. However, these local creeps are not going to run us out of town and destroy our credibility with future clients. Are you both still with me?"

"Absolutely," Clara said.

"I want to get the S.O.B. who shot my best friend. I'm not leaving until that is accomplished," Klahan agreed.

"Just remember that this could be a high-profile federal government program that we are poking a stick at, and the consequences could be dangerous."

"What is dangerous is that whoever shot John just pissed off a survivor of the Indo-China war called Vietnam.

They don't know the meaning of danger!" Daphne could see that Klahan was getting worked up and ready to kill anyone who threatened his best friend, much less took a shot at him.

"Klahan, we must let the local authorities deal with whomever shot John. Do you understand?" Daphne rarely gave Klahan specific instructions on how he should behave, but this was an exceptional time and place. She couldn't have Klahan going on a vengeful hunt for John's attacker and fouling up all the other plans that they had put in motion.

"I understand, Daphne. That doesn't mean I like it."

"Until we seal the fate of whoever is murdering these folks in Fairhope, we have to be cautious. Once that is accomplished, I could care less what happens to John's shooter." Klahan smiled knowingly and they moved on to how the investigation would work now that John was not able to help them.

"We need to set a trap for the murderer of Larry Washington and Jim Edmonds. If we happen to catch the person who shot John with the same techniques, all the better," Daphne said.

"How sure are you that the same person killed both men?" Klahan asked.

"I don't know that fact for sure, but all signs are pointing in that direction. And, if I'm correct about that assumption, it only makes sense that John was probably an additional assignment. In other words, get rid of the investigator and everything else settles out with a whimper."

“I must agree that your logic seems spot-on, but do we go with that assumption in our pursuit of the perp?” Clara asked.

“Absolutely not! I want you to go about these background investigations as if we know nothing about anything—let the chips fall where they may. Don’t let anything in the past influence your judgment on investigating anyone or anything. Our murderer may have had nothing to do with the proposed hit on John, but that would make shooting at an individual for no reason rather unusual and hardly believable. I just don’t want us to overlook anything large or small.” Daphne paused enough in her delivery to make sure both her investigators were totally on board with her thoughts. They both nodded affirmatively to indicate that they were listening to her and accepted her theories.

“I’m going to get John sent on his way tomorrow morning, and then the three of us need to get back together and plan our future moves,” Daphne said. “Both of you need to go to the hotel and get some sleep. It all starts over in the morning.”

* * *

True to her words, John was being released from the hospital at 9:00 AM, and the surgeon said he could go home and recuperate. Daphne didn’t want to take any chances with his recovery, so she sent him back to Daphne in an ambulance that she had privately hired, guaranteeing their fee both to and from Fairhope to Ashburn. She made John agree to take it easy and follow the doctor’s recommendations before she sent him on his way. Just to make sure he would not push the envelope Daphne had called Julie Anderson and a certified nursing assistant was standing by in Ashburn at their home/office to get John settled in and to check on his status a minimum of twice a day. John wasn't happy about leaving the job unfinished, but he really had no other choice but to go home and recover from his GSW. Daphne's parting words to John were lovingly stern. "Get your butt in bed when you get home and stay there until the doctor releases you from your post-operative trauma!"

"Yes, Dear," he could only say as the doors of the ambulance closed in his face. Daphne knew that if she had not sent him out of the area John would have tried to come back too soon, and that could have caused permanent damage to his internal organs. He complied with her requests, or should he say demands, but he didn't like it one bit. As the ambulance pulled away with its flashing lights illuminated, Daphne finally believed she could return to the case without worrying about John's care. Daphne saw the ambulance pull away from the hospital emergency room, and she drew a deep breath. While she was conflicted about having to work such an important case without her life-long partner, she was glad that he was safe and headed home to get well. Now the work would begin in earnest.

Chapter 13

A Wolf in Sheep's Clothing

Daphne had heard the phrase, "He's just a wolf in sheep's clothing" so many times in her life that she couldn't count. It was odd that their search of the truth had to go through one person—the very person who had hired the firm initially to dig for the truth in the murder of Larry Washington, the professional golfer. What did professional golf have to do with anything in this case? Was it a coincidence that Washington was brutally attacked in a place and manner that usually depicted rest and recuperation? Were Washington and Jim Edmonds friends, or connected some other way in business? Were there similarities to the deaths, and if so, what were they? All these questions were whirling through Daphne's mind as she went back to the Fairhope Inn to rest and rethink their approach to the fear that had overtaken Fairhope. As she was checking into the room, she saw Clara and Klahan sitting outside in the small restaurant garden area having a cocktail. She thought it might be good to join them and bring them up to date on John's situation, speak to them about their next steps in the investigation, and get the ball rolling again. What Daphne didn't want to do was let any leads grow cold on John's shooting, Jim Edmonds' murder, or Larry Washington's demise. They needed to determine if any or all of those events were linked somehow. She approached their table with a big smile.

"We finally have John headed back to the safety of Ashburn, and now it's left to the three of us to figure out what is going on in Fairhope. Do either of you have a clue as to how to move forward?"

"I think we may have stumbled upon something interesting in Mayor Jackson's background," Klahan said. "It appears that Jackson and Edmonds served in the same military outfit in Afghanistan, and all records of their service have been expunged or redacted. I'm thinking it has something to do with Edmonds' death. I still don't know how the golf pro is involved, if he is, and how to tie that murder to the suspiciousness of Jackson's and Edmonds' relationship. We're still digging on that one."

"Interesting," Daphne said. "How about you, Clara. Anything turn up yet on our mysterious mayor?"

"Nothing mysterious. However, I did some cross-checking on financial institutions and investments, and I found several banks and corporations where both Edmonds and the mayor were investors. That by itself is not mysterious or even suspicious, but the death of Edmonds puts a different light on the investigation. My next step is to see if Larry Washington had any dealings with the mayor or Edmonds. I should know something about any connections between the three men sometime this afternoon. If they are connected by investment portfolios, then we may have something to go on. Right now, it's all just conjecture!"

"Stay on that potential lead, and Klahan and I will refocus on the mayor. With that much smoke, there must be a fire somewhere!" Daphne said. They all agreed on the plan moving forward, Daphne got up and headed to her room, and Klahan and Clara decided to grab a bite of lunch before resuming their investigations. While they were just grabbing for straws, things were beginning to come together somewhat, and there was promise that all the events of recent days in Fairhope might be linked together.

As Daphne was entering her room, she noticed the message light on her telephone was blinking, indicating that someone had tried to call her. She hoped whoever it had been had left a message. Picking up the receiver and dialing the front desk, she found out that Colonel Rocky Crawford had left a message for her. That peeked her interest, and she immediately placed a call to his office at the police department. After a few moments she was connected to him in his office.

"This is Chief Crawford. How may I help you?"

"Chief Crawford, this is Daphne Whitacre. I am returning your phone call. I missed your call at my hotel, and I wanted to know why you were trying to contact me."

"Yes, Daphne. Thanks for returning my call. We just got the ballistics report back on the shell casing that was found near the scene of your husband's shooting. It appears to be a Russian made, Kalashnikov AK-47 rifle, issued to Cuban forces sometime in the late 1970s. So far that's all we know, but the 7.62x39mm rounds don't lie. How and why it made its way to Fairhope, Alabama, is still a mystery, but we have some ideas about that."

"Such as?"

"I don't want to speculate at this time, but it is suspected that a crate of Kalashnikov rifles were lost in a shipment from Russia to Cuba some years ago. None of them have surfaced until now. We have a way of tracking that shipment, with the help of a former enemy, and we hope to have more definite information soon. I will call you when I know more. For now, it appears that Organized Crime may be involved in your husband's shooting. We aren't sure about the other two murders at this time, but we will continue to investigate until we can either prove they are or are not connected to the attempt on Mr. Bremen's life."

"Thanks, Chief. I will listen for your call." Daphne hung up the phone and pondered what she had just been told. How and why would a Cuban AK-47 be connected with John's attempted assassination, and did that indicate someone connected with Cuba and organized crime was involved? This investigation was getting very convoluted, and what had seemed like a possible vendetta against a former C.I.A. operative was now much more likely a larger attempt to prevent a previous crime from being reported. Daphne would call John later and get his input on the new facts. John had been very involved with F.B.I. investigations of the domestic Mafia in the past, and the indicators that the C.I.A. might have evidence of a Cuban Mafia affiliation might have similar connections. John and Klahan were experts when it came to identifying and hunting down Mafia leads—that's what they did for years when John was the Director of the F.B.I. Office in Dallas, Texas. Daphne didn't want to get ahead of herself, but these recent leads by Chief Crawford might develop into something meaningful. Still, she had to wonder how that might tie Mayor Jackson to the murder of the golf pro, Jim Edmonds' killing, and the attempt on her husband's life. She picked up the phone and called Clara.

"Are you and Klahan still together?"

"Yes. Is there something you need to tell us?"

"Definitely. Where are you two?"

"We're still in the restaurant having some lunch. Do you want us to come to you or do you want to come to us?"

"When you and Klahan have finished your lunch please come by my room. We need to discuss some information that I just was given by Police Chief Rocky Crawford." Clara agreed, and they decided to forego anything else to eat or drink, paid the check, and headed to Daphne's room. Their interest was piqued about this new revelation. They walked to the desk, got Daphne's room number from the clerk, and headed down the first-floor hallway.

"Come in," Daphne said as she ushered them into her room. "Do you guys want a drink?"

"No, we just finished lunch. What's so compelling that we need to know about before we begin determining the details of the last few days." Klahan asked. "It was obvious to Daphne that he wanted to get to work on his investigation without any more delays.

"It may be nothing, but it may be something very important," Daphne said. She watched Klahan as she shared Colonel Crawford's news. "Let me ask you a question, Klahan. What rifle or weapon would you say was the Mafia's preference, assuming they had a choice?"

"That's easy. Either a M-4 Carbine or an AK-47."

"Why not an AR-15?" Clara asked.

"Basically, because the M-4 Carbine and the AK-47 are fully automatic, and while it is illegal to use them that way in the United States, the Mafia never worries about legality when it comes to weapons and their use."

"Does the M-4 and an AK-47 use the same ammo?"

"Nope. The M-4 uses 5.62x45mm rounds, while the AK-47 uses 7.62x39mm ammunition. They both are accurate up to about 500 meters, but neither is as accurate as the M-16, which was adapted from the AR-15 strictly for military use—in other words for war theatres."

"Why doesn't the Mafia use M-16s?"

"They would if they could get them, along with the spare parts and ammunition for them. There have been some cases where soldiers in the field have smuggled their trusty M-16 back into the country in their baggage, but it's rare."

"Why do you think it is more accurate than the M-4 or the AK-47?"

"First of all, it's much lighter, it fires a smaller round, and if kept dry and free of dirt and sand, it will work until the barrel gets so hot you cannot hold it. Unfortunately, the Monsoon rains in Southeast Asia and excessive sand that they were exposed to made them less than perfect for jungle fighting. The thought was to make then light, since the stock and other parts were mainly plastic, the only weight to the weapon is the barrel, the ammo clip, and the bayonet that one might strap to the end of the rifle."

"The AK-47 is better? Is that what I'm hearing?"

"The AK-47 has a wooden stock and can be fired after being buried in the sand and water—especially a Kalashnikov AK-47."

"You just lost me."

"There are two major manufacturers of AK-47 rifles, the Communist Chinese AK-47, which is a variant of the original weapon, and the Russian Kalashnikov AK-47. Mikhail Kalashnikov designed the weapon in 1945, and it has become the most popular military rifle of all time. Now, over twenty countries make some variants of the same weapon. By and large, the Russian AK-47 is the best ever made."

"Now that's a primer on weapons of war!" Clara laughed. "I feel like I know more about weapons of war than I ever thought I would! How did you find out all of that information?" Klahan took a deep breath, looked at Daphne, and began his life story.

"Are you sure you want to hear this story?" he asked.

"I know very little about you and your history. I'm intrigued to learn more about my associates whom I depend on day-to-day to protect my six."

"Here goes. I was born in Bangkok, Thailand, lived there with my family until I was a teen, and moved to the City of Hua, South Vietnam, with my parents. They were both professors at the University of Hue, just south of the Demilitarized Zone, and were murdered by the Viet Cong when I was still in high school. I grew up just trying to survive the Viet Cong, because my folks and I were on a death list by the North Vietnamese Regulars, and I eventually made my way to Saigon, South Vietnam, and there I met my best friend and savior, John Bremen." Clara noticed that Klahan had become very quiet as he recalled his past years in Saigon. She was going to tell Klahan that it wasn't important for him to continue his story, but he began again, and Clara couldn't find a place to interrupt his story.

"Anyway, the Viet Cong and North Vietnamese Regulars both used Chicom AK-47s as their main weapon of choice. I became very familiar with that weapon, basically because I needed to know how to use it to survive in a hostile climate. John introduced me to other weapons, took me under his wing as an orphaned South Vietnamese youth, and we became the best of friends. In fact, in 1975 John had me smuggled out of Saigon before the U.S. Embassy was overrun by the enemy. I have no doubt that he saved my life! He had me flown to Bangkok, then on to the United States. We have been inseparable partners ever since. That's how and why I became so familiar with weapons of war." He looked at Clara who was sitting with her mouth agape—she had never heard such a fantastic story about someone she actually knew.

"Back to Daphne's question about which weapon the Mafia preferred—I would have to say the AK-47. They are virtually indestructible, while at the same time somewhat crude in their construction. Since so many of them were made for war, they are still plentiful and the ammunition for them is available in large quantities. Why do you ask?"

"Colonel Crawford just informed me that the shell casings that were found near the area where John was attacked were 7.62 caliber, and he thinks they were standard AK-47 ammunition." She waited for his reaction, which came quickly.

"Well, I'll be a S.O.B.! Does he suspect it to be a Russian AK-47?"

"More interesting than that!" Klahan looked at Daphne with confusion showing on his face. "Guess who Crawford thinks manufactured the weapon that was fired at John." Klahan just raised his hands in a gesture of frustration. "He thinks it was a Cuban AK-47. Probably shipped to Cuba sometime in the 1970s after the Bay of Pigs confrontation."

"You must be kidding! Cuban? The Cubans are involved in whatever is going on in Fairhope?"

"Don't jump to any conclusions yet! You and Clara are going to have to dig even deeper now that we think there may be a Mafia connection with Cuban influence involved in one or more of the murders."

"That does make things more interesting," Clara said. "Don't worry Daphne. Klahan and I are up to the task."

"John and I are counting on both of you to get the job done. If the Mafia is somehow involved in this mess, we have a totally different scenario than when we first began the investigation. I want you and Clara to work out of her Fairhope office and try to see if you can tie any of this to the Mafia or some other entity in Cuba. I know it sounds weird, but it is the first real lead we've had."

"We will get on it and let you know what we can piece together. Are you going to tell John what's happening?" Klahan asked.

"In good time, Klahan—in good time."

Chapter 14

Behind the Veil

Merriam Webster defines a veil as "*a piece of opaque or transparent material worn over the face for concealment, for protection from the elements, or to enhance the appearance.*" One might be hiding behind a veil for various reasons, but definitely to prevent being recognized in public. If Klahan's and Clara's investigation revealed that someone in the Cuban Mafia, or someone with Communist ties to Cuba, were involved in the three incidents in Fairhope, then the investigation could spiral out into an international embarrassment for whomever was involved. In other words, this investigation had just become much more sensitive in nature. The question was who was hiding behind the veil of disinformation that kept getting in the way of discovering who was really behind the deaths of Larry Washington and Jim Edmonds, and why? When Daphne and her investigators were able to determine whom that might be, they would be much closer to the truth. Daphne had called Klahan and Clara and asked them to meet her on the patio for lunch. When they arrived Klahan had an idea that he wanted to bounce off Daphne.

"Daphne, I still have some contact with the Senior Advisor of SOUTHCOM, the F.B.I.'s southern command in Miami. Of course he wasn't there for the Bay of Pigs fiasco, but he has done a lot of study on what happened, and why it failed. His name is Harry Lawrence, and he has a history of working in the law enforcement industry and as a military liaison. Just some of his specialties are law enforcement, surveillance, counterterrorism, and physical security. He has studied the failed invasion of our troops and why he thinks that their secret attack on Cuba was leaked from our own troops. He would be a good person to verify the validity of the AK-47, whether it is a vintage weapon of the kind used during the Cuban invasion or not. I'll give him a call and see if he can join us. I am guessing you'd prefer to have him come here, rather than have me take the weapon's casing to him in Miami."

"I doubt you can board an aircraft that would fly you to Miami with an AK-47 cartridge in your checked baggage!" Daphne laughed. "I know you still have lots of contacts in the government, but even you can't pull that off!"

"You're right. Only a magician could pull that off. I'm sure if we agreed to pay his way here, put him up in the Fairhope Inn, bought him a nice dinner or two with drinks, that he would agree to help. His pay will go on whether he is working with us or staying in Miami, so we'd only be responsible for his expenses. What do you say?"

"Give him a call and see what he thinks about coming to Fairhope. You or Clara could drive over to Mobile and pick him up at the airport."

"If he agrees to come, he may have access to a private plane that could land at H.L. Sonny Callahan Airport in Fairhope. From what I understand, the airport has a 6,600-foot-long runway, more than capable of landing a small corporate jet. Depending on his authority and the Miami F.B.I. Office's ability to commandeer aircraft for investigative purposes, he may be able to make his own arrangements to land locally. Let me talk to him and see what he thinks. If he can tie that AK-47 to the time of the Cuban invasion and/or the Mafia operating in Cuba then we will definitely have a new direction to search for answers."

"It's worth a call. Let me know how much it's going to cost us to bring him to Fairhope. I'm not worried about room, food, and drinks—an aircraft rental is in a different realm!"

"I understand. I'll call him and let you know." Klahan excused himself to make the call to the Miami F.B.I. Office. He didn't know Harry Lawrence well, but the F.B.I. was like a big fraternity. Once you were a member, you maintained certain privileges for life. If Harry could help Klahan and John Bremen solve a crime that involved slowing the growth of the Mafia, he would probably try to help.

"Clara let's kick your counter-personality, Lucy Ledbetter, into gear, and let's see how much dirt Mayor Todd Jackson has under his fingernails! I find it very coincidental that both murders relating to our case have overtones of influence by the mayor. The mayor is the principal owner, mover and shaker, of the Rocky Creek Golf Club, and Jim Edmonds was one of his best friends. Adding to that fact, both Jackson and Edmonds served in the same military outfit where all their history is now either redacted or 'eyes-only.' It makes one wonder if our good mayor may still be actively involved in something clandestine."

"I'd say that's an accurate statement. From what I have experienced over the years in my investigation in Cullman, when one begins turning over rocks things become more evident and damning. However, if Jackson is connected with the federal government for reasons other than legitimate ones, we might be stirring up a hornet's nest. Are you ready for those results?"

"If we get that kind of reaction from the feds then we will have even more reason to pursue the mayor. Of course, there is nothing to keep the government from pulling 'National Security' reasons for shutting down our investigation."

"With two high-profile deaths evident to the general public, it will be difficult for anyone to quell this investigation for any reason."

"OK. Do your best to stir things up a bit, and let's let the chips fall where they may!" Daphne said. "I need to give John a call and bring him up to date on what has happened and tell him how we plan to move forward." Clara left the table and headed for her new office down the street.

Daphne needed to bring her husband, best friend, and partner in their detective agency up to date on what had been decided by the three of them. He might also have some insights into moving forward with the help of the F.B.I. After all, he had been the Dallas F.B.I. Office Director for some time before retiring to start their own detective agency. She dialed the number for the office.

"You've reached the Bremen and Whitacre Detective Agency. How may we help you?" Julie Anderson said when she answered the phone.

"Julie, this is Daphne. How are things there? Is John in this afternoon?"

"Oh, yes. He most certainly is in the office." Daphne heard stress in the reply by their office manager and gate keeper.

"Is he bugging you?" Daphne asked with a laugh.

“Uh-huh,” was the only thing Julie could say without giving away their conversation to John, who was sitting just a few feet away from Julie. It was obvious to Daphne that John needed a mission. Otherwise, he would drive Julie out of her mind until he could get back out in the field.

“Let me speak to him.”

“This is John. Who am I speaking with?” was the question he put forth to Daphne, not knowing it was she calling into the office.

“John, this is Daphne. How are you?”

“I’m fine, but I need to be involved in this investigation, and I don’t think there is any reason I can’t be doing more to help!” Daphne could hear the frustration in his voice, and she knew him better than anyone.

“You’re in luck! We think we may have a new lead that you can help us research there from the office.”

“Let’s hear about it. I’m about to go stir-crazy sitting here waiting for the telephone to ring.”

“According to the local police department that recovered the shell casings from the rifle, which was used to attack you, the weapon appears to be an AK-47, of Russian manufacturing. And get this. It very well be one of a number of AK-47s that were confiscated during the Bay of Pigs Invasion attempt in the 1960s.”

“Like the ones that the Cuban Mafia used when they moved their operations to the United States? That’s been over 50 years ago. What do you think that means?”

"I'll ask you the same question. Do you think the Mafia is involved in our murder plots in Fairhope, and if so, how is Mayor Jackson tied to all of it? Is he also a victim, or is he part of the problem?"

"You came up with all of this in less than a day?" John marveled.

"Well, I had some speculative help. Klahan agreed that everything was too coincidental for something like this to happen without someone or some organization being behind it. He has a friend in the Miami F.B.I. Office who may come to Fairhope to identify the weapon and give us further insights on how the Mafia might be involved."

"Who?"

"Do you remember Harry Lawrence? According to Klahan, Harry is very informed on all things related to Cuban infiltration into our country. I've never heard you speak of him from your experiences in the F.B.I. when you were running the Dallas office."

"We attended some meetings together back in the day, but I never had any specific missions with him or anyone in his office. From what I remember of him is that he is one of the best minds we have when it comes to the Mafia in the Miami area. However, when we were investigated the Mafia in New Orleans and other areas in the South, we always believed the key to the Mafia involvement in our areas was coming from the New Orleans Mafia family."

"Klahan believes that Harry can arrange to fly directly into Fairhope on a small private jet, and we will only be liable for his room and food while he is here. I told Klahan to make it happen." Daphne and John always discussed things of this nature in the past, but she believed that he would understand that time was of the essence and would not fault her in taking action before discussing it with him.

"Great decision, Partner," John reassured her. "I never doubted you could make good decisions without me. I just never wanted to feel anything but needed!

"Oh, you are needed! I want you to get well so you can get back out in the field with me. However, I want you to be fully healed and ready to charge into a burning building, as usual!" Although John couldn't see Daphne, he knew she had a big smile on her face when she added the last comment.

"OK. I need to go. Clara and I are working the local aspect of investigating the mayor, while Klahan is making the arrangements to get Harry Lawrence here. I'll check in later today. And, by the way, why don't you take a walk on the Quadrangle on the Ashburn University Campus and give Julie a break?"

"You think I may be getting on her nerves?"

"Maybe," was all she said. He hung up and told Julie that he would be out of the office for a while. He noticed that she seemed to let out a sigh as he left the office for his extended walk on the campus.

John and Daphne had bought the old mansion across from the Ashburn University Campus Quadrangle, known locally as the QUAD, when they came back to Ashburn some years ago. The mansion had a colorful history, to include a missing heiress whose body had been found in a secret passageway in the basement some years before John and Daphne bought the old place. It was huge.

There were three floors, over six-thousand square feet, bedrooms and bathrooms on the top two floors, and converted office space on the main floor for their detective agency. Clara was living on the third floor in an apartment created for her when she joined the agency after retiring from the Cullman Police Department. There also was a wraparound covered porch with rocking chairs that pointed to the West, toward the QUAD. However, when John was in the office, his presence was large enough to intimidate Julie while she was trying to carry on the day-to-day business. Although Julie loved John and Daphne, she preferred to have the office to herself when possible.

* * *

Klahan placed the call to Harry Lawrence in Miami, and he was pleasantly surprised that Harry had remembered him from Klahan's stint with the agency in Dallas. They had never worked directly together in the past, but he Klahan had made a name for himself by running a very efficient and successful office. Klahan's office had cleaned up many Mafia strongholds during his tenure in Dallas, and Harry had been a silent fan of Klahan's success.

"I would love to help you in any way I can," Harry said. "What do you need?"

Klahan filled Harry in on his move to the detective field after his retirement from the F.B.I., told him about John's and Daphne's successes, and moved on to the purpose of his call.

"Harry, we have discovered something very odd in one of our investigations, and we thought it might also hold interest for the Miami F.B.I. We are willing to put you up in a local hotel in Fairhope, Alabama, if you can get away for a few days and give us your input into our investigation." Klahan told Harry about the Cuban AK-47, a little bit about the assassination attempt on John, and tied it all up nicely suggesting that the local Mafia might be involved. He asked Harry what he would need to come to Fairhope.

"Let me get back with you. Give me an hour." Harry hung up, and Klahan crossed his fingers and held his breath. If he had done a good job, he might get Harry to come to Fairhope on the F.B.I.'s expense account, and not on the Bremen and Whitacre expense account. Klahan called Daphne and brought her up to date on the conversation. True to his word, Harry returned Klahan's call an hour later.

"Klahan, here's what I can do. I understand that there is an airport in the Fairhope area. According to my information, it will accommodate a Gulf Stream G4, which we happen to have available in our hanger. I can fly into the area tomorrow morning, spend the day with you and your team, and fly back out tomorrow night. There will be no cost to you or your team, as we have had those Cuban AK-47s on our radar for some time. This is not the first time a Cuban AK-47 has turned up in a murder-for-hire plot in the Southern United States. That's why I can justify my trip at no cost to you. However, if we need to spend more in Fairhope, or commit more people to the task, we can cross that bridge when we come to it. Right now, this is not part of an F.B.I. investigation, and I know you realized the importance of us officially staying out of the investigation as long as possible. If you turn up definite Mafia involvement somewhere in your future investigation, we may need to step in and take control. I can hold the

F.B.I. off until you get your case solved. I'll promise you that much. What do you think?"

"Come on!" Klahan said without hesitation. "I'll let John and Daphne know about your trip to Fairhope tomorrow." Klahan hung up knowing that he had accomplished his primary goal of getting help from the F.B.I. without them trying to take over the investigation. That could have killed the private investigation of the Bremen and Whitacre Agency, and that could have cost them lots of money. He called Daphne, got her to agree to get John on a conference call with Klahan, Clara, and herself, so he wouldn't have to explain the conditions of the F.B.I.'s help but one time.

"Is everyone on board?" Klahan asked. He heard John, Daphne, and Clara all answer in the affirmative. "I want to share some good news. I just spoke with a previous acquaintance of mine and John's at the F.B.I. His name is Harry Lawrence, and he is charge of the Mafia related information gathering branch in the Miami F.B.I. Office. He remembers me and John, and he has his own interest in running down the origin of the Cuban AK-47 which was used to try an assassinate John the other day. He is willing to fly to Fairhope on his own Gulfstream G4, spend the day with us, and charge us nothing for his time or expenses. The only caveat is that if we turn up definite traceable Cuban AK-47 connections with the local Mafia, we eventually give the Miami F.B.I. the opportunity to follow up on the case, but not until we have finished our investigation. How does that sound to everyone?"

"That sounds great, Klahan," John was the first to comment and congratulate his old partner on a job well done. "When's he flying into Fairhope?"

"Tomorrow morning. I suggest that I pick him up and that the three of us meet with him at the Fairhope Inn for an informal query. I'm sure he will have questions that I can't answer without Clara and Daphne's input. Will that work for you ladies?" They both confirmed that the next morning would be fine. They agreed to meet around 10:00 AM, and they ended the call.

* * *

Klahan was waiting on the tarmac as the Gulfstream G4 landed and taxied to the waiting car that Klahan had rented for their use while Harry was in town. He had rented a no-nonsense, black ford sedan with no bells and whistles. The last thing Klahan wanted to do was alert the local authorities that he had invited the F.B.I. into the investigation of a local matter without the invitation of the local constabulary, which was a big no-no. The F.B.I. was usually invited into a local investigation when the local police department believed that their investigation was beyond the abilities of their local office's capabilities. However, no one in the Bremen and Whitacre Agency had the authority to alert the F.B.I. of anything, much less invite them to join in an investigation. Klahan figured forgiveness would be easier to get than permission, and he really didn't care if possible corrupt local authorities got their feelings hurt. It wasn't a proven fact that the local constabulary was corrupted in any way, but there was always that possibility. The simple fact that the deed was done, and he would live with whatever consequences came from his decision. John and Daphne thought it was a good idea to bring Harry into the mix, so Klahan couldn't be bothered about anyone else's concerns. John saw a tall, thin man deplane the small jetliner, and walk directly toward him on the tarmac.

“Are you Klahan?” Harry asked, his hand extended in a gesture of friendship.

“I am. You must be Harry Lawrence.” Klahan was viewing a slim man, six-feet tall, with a confident stride as he approached.

“What was the giveaway? The suit or the G4?” Harry smiled.

“Both,” Klahan said. “We get very few suits in Fairhope, and I can’t remember any Gulfstream G4s. However, I’m sure some of the millionaires in the local vicinity have Gulfstream jets hangered in these secure facilities,” Klahan indicated the many closed hangars that skirted the main runway. “We’re glad to see you. This case has definitely been a challenge.” Harry had no baggage, so Klahan put Harry’s briefcase in the backseat of the sedan, and they headed from the small airport to the Fairhope Inn. Harry’s flight had arrived at 9:00 AM local time, so they had time to get the small group together for the 10:00 AM planned meeting at the hotel. Klahan filled Harry in on as many facts as he was able to recall off the top of his head as they drove to the Fairhope Inn.

“Wow, this is a beautiful town,” Harry commented as they drove down the tree-lined streets. “Some of these Water oaks appear to be a hundred of years old or more.”

“According to locals, some of these trees were here when Fairhope and Mobile were still American Indian Territory. I don’t know if that’s fact or fiction, but there is a lot of history in this part of the United States. It’s a historical fact that the Spanish landed in the Mobile Bay area in the early 1500s, but they moved on to the West and eventually landed in Baha California and the Southwestern

United States around San Diego and Los Angeles. Then just west of here you have the controversial "Coonass" people of South Mississippi and Louisiana. This area was originally settled by the French in the 17th century, and the customs of the French, mixed with the local uneducated people, resulted in a culture with its own language and lifestyle. The Mafia has had its tenacles deeply rooted in this part of the Southern United States for many years. We thought the Cuban AK-47 might have some connection to those people or the Mafia which operates there. That's our area in a nutshell."

"That's a lot of information that I didn't possess before landing. Our first goal will be to trace the weapon you believe was used to try an assassinate John Bremen. Beyond that, I don't have a precise plan. We'll let things play out as things happen. If it is indeed a Cuban AK-47, someone high up in the hierarchy of the local Mafia family will be upset that they got dragged into something as messy as murder with contraband weapons. I know you've had dealings with the Mafia when you worked in the Dallas F.B.I. Office, so we both know how structured and disciplined the Mafia can be. Someone's head may be displaced after making such a mistake of using an almost forgotten weapon to eliminate an enemy."

"My thoughts exactly." They pulled up in front of the quaint Fairhope Inn. Klahan parked the car on the street and indicated for Harry to move to the covered patio that was part of the Fairhope Inn Restaurant. They took chairs and Klahan called Clara and Daphne and asked them to come to the patio to meet Harry. In what seemed like minutes, both Clara and Daphne appeared. Harry stood up to greet them, shook their hands, and sat back down.

"It's good to meet your entire team," Harry said. "How may I be of assistance?"

"We are missing a very important part of the team, but I'm going to get him on the phone and put him on the speaker so he can take part in this session." Daphne dialed John's number and waited for him to answer. John picked up the call and they all were ready to learn what they could from a true veteran of the wars with the Mafia.

Chapter 14

Moving Parts

After ordering coffee and pastries, Daphne used the time to bring Harry up to date on everything that they had to date about both murders, along with the information Klahan had already shared with Harry about the suspected Cuban AK-47. Daphne showed Harry the coroner's report on the caliber of the round taken from John's wound, and she pointed out the consistency that it had with 7.62 caliber AK-47 ammunition. After hearing all the information, Harry confirmed what everyone already knew. The weapon used to assault John Bremen was an AK-47, and from the casings found at the scene, it was apparently a Russian Kalashnikov model, similar to the ones sent to Cuba during the Cuban Missile Conflict in the early 1960s. It was no secret that the AK-47 was the favorite weapon of choice for most third-world countries, both because they were inexpensive to manufacture, and the ammunition was plentiful throughout the world. Originally manufactured by the Soviet Union in 1949, they were now manufactured all over the world, and there were more than seventy-two million in use somewhere in the world at any one time. While they were not the most accurate weapon of choice, they were affordable for the average drug cartel, or for the demagog who wished to overthrow his duly elected government, and also for collectors of automatic weapons. However, there were only a few hundred Russian AK-47 shipped to Cuba in the early 1960s in support of Fidel Castro's coup against the Batista Family, and if the AK-47 used to try and assassinate John was one of those weapons, it was a pretty good bet that the underground and corrupt forces at work in the Cuban government at the time had sold those weapons to the Mafia. Once the Mafia decided that moving from Cuba to the Southern United States posed a much better climate for their nefarious deeds, they simple brought those weapons with them when they moved West.

"Harry, what do you think it means if the weapon used to wound John was or is owned by the Mafia?" Harry thought for a moment, resting his face in his right hand as he pondered Daphne's question.

"It could mean nothing at all, or it might mean that the Mafia is somehow tied to the two murders you discussed earlier."

"You don't think it could be coincidental that someone passed an AK-47 to a hood who was trying to protect his own criminal enterprise?"

"Do you believe in coincidences when it comes to someone being attacked with an AK-47? I surely don't think so. No, I think you need to get to the bottom of who owns the weapon in question and why it was used in an attempt upon John's life."

"Do you have any suggestions as to how to approach such an investigation to the ownership of an antique AK-47? Obviously, it won't be registered with the Bureau of Alcohol, Tobacco, Firearms, and Explosions, or we could just look up the ownership in the registry of weapons."

"There is one thing that may help you with the ATF. They have a list of all illegally trafficked assault weapons that date back to the turn of the century. So, if we can locate the actual AK-47 used in the attempt on John's life, and assuming the serial number is still intact on the barrel, we can determine if it is one of the missing weapons that was originally sent to Cuba from Russian over 50 years ago."

"Yes, but how do we go about finding the weapon?"

"How do we always locate the hard-to-find stuff?" Harry waited for Daphne to take the bait, and then he smiled. As she answered he nodded his head in agreement.

"Follow the money!" Daphne said. From the telephone they all heard John agree with his wife and long-time partner.

"The man has a point, Daphne. Let's see if we can do a little more digging on the mayor and see if he has any moving parts we haven't discovered yet.

* * *

Klahan took Harry back to the Fairhope Airport, watched him board the Gulfstream G4, and then watched it gracefully lift off the end of the runway on its way back to Miami. Harry had only been in Fairhope a few hours, from touchdown to takeoff, but he had put them on a serious path to discovering the origin of the weapon use to shoot John Bremen. On his way back from the airport, Klahan received a phone call from Daphne.

"Yeah, Daphne. What's up? I got Harry on his way back to Miami. What do you want me to do now?"

"Go directly to Lucy Ledbetter's Insurance Agency office in Fairhope. We need to expedite our search on the financial empire of Mayor Jackson. Clara has been lining things up while you were taking Harry back to his plane, but now she can use some help running down some leads, both locally and off-shore."

"Got it. I'm on my way." In a matter of minutes Klahan was parking the sedan in front of Clara's fictitious detective agency office. He went inside, pulled up a chair in front of one of the desktop computers, and asked how he might help.

"I am contacting all the local banks, lenders, and savings and loan companies in the immediate area, to include the Mobile, Alabama, locations. What I could use from you is help in contacting the notorious offshore institutions where the crooks and thieves hide their ill-gotten gains from the government's watchful eyes. I have a common list of those companies you can begin with." Clara passed Klahan a list of names of banks to call, and he began his task without delay. They both worked for a couple of hours before they came up for air. Clara declared that they needed a break, so she and Klahan got a cup of coffee and sat in the arrangement of chairs set up for their fictitious clients' visits. After a few moments of quiet contemplation, Klahan spoke firmly.

"I'm not sure what you found, Clara, but what I discovered was a myriad of convoluted transactions where money was apparently moved from one offshore account to another. Fortunately, in my past years as Director of the F.B.I. Office in Dallas, Texas, I have seen such transactions before. Each deposit, transfer, and withdrawal leaves a footprint that can be traced, assuming the person tracing the movements is familiar with the mechanics of the actions being taken. I have that kind of experience, so I can probably find most, if not all, of any subterfuge in the accounting practices of Mayor Todd Jackson."

"That's great!" she said. "How is that possible, assuming there is no accountability to the United States Treasury Department required by offshore banking companies?"

"We don't use the banks for our tracking sources. Rather, we use the electronic signatures, footprints, and coordinating of cell phone transactions that can be pinpointed by triangulation of associated transmission towers."

"That's too complicated for my simple mind to grasp, but I'll take your word for it. How long will it take to run down the movement of the money to all the hiding spots?"

"I will need to get Daphne to authorize me to spend a little money to hire a special team to do all the calculations, but it can be done in a matter of hours, assuming the person doing the searching knows what to do and has the equipment to accomplish the task."

"I'm sure she'll be happy to spend the money if it will help lead to whomever shot John and killed the other two poor souls."

"What did you discover from your local search?" Klahan asked.

"Multiple and somewhat questionable transfers of money in the amounts just under the $10,000 federal level that has to be reported by each financial institution. Since the 911 incident, every domestic transfer of money, even from one personal account to another, that exceeds $10,000 *must* be reported to the federal government."

"That's not a crime, though," Klahan said.

"No, but I found one local bank where $9800 was transferred fifty-eight times in less than one month on Mayor Jackson's personal banking accounts. What does that indicate to you?"

"Either that he is depositing ill-gotten gains into his accounts, transferring it around, or trying to launder it somehow through banks and lending institutions."

"Exactly! I'm getting a printout from each bank sent to me, of which there are four in the Fairhope area, as well as three other ones in the Mobile area."

"None in Mississippi or Florida?"

"No, it seems Mayor Jackson is smart enough to know that once money is transferred across state lines the penalty for getting caught for laundering money is much greater than just intrastate offenses. The federal government penalties are not the kind where parole is often offered, compared to individual states where housing non-violent criminals gets little support or attention."

"Well, we knew the mayor was smart, didn't we? I've no doubt he has been fronting for some bad stuff for years, but that's not our concern unless it leads us to the demise of two innocent victims and the near death of our friend John Bremen!"

"Klahan, why don't you give Daphne a call, let her fill John in on what we've discovered, and see if she will authorize your expedited form of research of those offshore accounts. I'll be very surprised if she doesn't jump at it." Klahan agreed, walked outside of the office, and made a call to Daphne. The call was just being answered when Klahan dropped his cell phone and stooped down to pick it up off the sidewalk. A shot rang out and a projectile hit the brick wall behind Klahan at head level. If he had not dropped his phone he might be dead. Klahan picked up the phone and hustled back inside the office quickly, turned off the lights, grabbed Clara from her desk, and headed for the backdoor.

"What's going on, Klahan?" Clara asked with a surprised look on her face. "Where are we going, and why are we going there so quickly?"

"Evidently you didn't hear the shot outside."
"What shot?"

"Exactly! Someone took a shot at me as I stood in front of this office trying to make a cell phone call to Daphne. Fortunately for me, the phone slipped out of my pocket and hit the ground. As I picked it up to replace the call I heard a rifle shot ring out and saw some brick dust fly off the wall head high behind me. Someone was trying to shoot me in the head, and if I hadn't had not fumbled my cell phone I would be lying in a pool of blood with a hole in my head!" Clara looked at him with a renewed horror.

"What do we do?"

"I noticed when I was here the last time that you had a backdoor that opened into the alley for potential deliveries. We will carefully exit through the door, move carefully to the main street, and get back to the Fairhope Inn. There was no mistake about the intentions of whoever was shooting at me. They wanted me dead."

"I guess that means that our cover is blown."

"Yeah, I'd agree with that summation. The question for me is who wants us dead and how did they find out about our cover story? I don't believe that either of us doubt who might be behind this action, do we?"

"Not a chance. The mayor is going to pay for taking a shot at us. I can promise you that!"

"I'd rather see him in prison in the general population than for one of us to kick his butt. Let's make that happen."

"I'm with you, Klahan. How do we determine who outed us?"

"Thanks to my F.B.I. training that's easier than you might imagine." As soon as Klahan believed that he and Clara were out of the immediate danger of being shot by a sniper he called Daphne and filled her in on what happened. She suggested that they meet somewhere for dinner to discuss future actions that they needed to take, and Daphne wasn't sure if the phones in the Fairhope Inn were compromised. Her cell phone was secure, but she needed to see her agents face-to-face at this point.

"Let's meet at Gambino's on South Mobile Street. You are about six or seven blocks north of the restaurant. They open at 5 PM, and I'll call and make a reservation for an early seating. I'll walk from here and meet you both there in a matter of ten minutes or so. Since it's already 5:00 PM, you should have no problem getting in and seated. If you beat me there, go ahead and get us a table. The reservations will be in the name of Delores Banks."

"Delores Banks? Who the hell is Delores Banks?"

"I'll tell you at dinner. See you soon!" Daphne hung up the phone and freshened up for her dinner date. This was getting to be very exciting, even though they were being personally attacked on all sides by someone, probably the mayor. She and John had never run from a fight in their professional careers, and this was not going to be the first time for such an event to happen. It was curious to her how Lucy Ledbetter's cover was outed. She guessed she'd find out as time went by, but she had a strong suspicion of who might be behind the leak. Ready now for dinner, Daphne put on her walking shoes and headed for Gambino's. How perfectly appropriate for them to being planning how to reveal the secrets of the Mafia while eating in a splendid Italian restaurant.

Chapter 15

The Master Plan

Gambino's Restaurant was not your typical Fairhope restaurant that catered to the well-financed retirees who frequented the small city each year during the summer months for vacations. It had a reputation as being an authentic Italian restaurant, fully established as *the* place to eat at night for a full experience of the old county cuisine normally only found in Italy itself. The waitstaff spoke little English, but were fluent in Italian and Spanish, presenting the optics of one really being in a ristorante in Florence or Rome, not on the banks of Mobile Bay. Customs that normally occurred in Italy reoccurred in Gambino's on a regular basis. Ordering coffee at Gambino's was either a Caffe or a Cappuccino, and the later was never to be ordered after lunch or dinner—it was understood that cappuccino was a breakfast drink. Cornetto or a brioche was how one would order a truly Italian croissant, and Spremuta d' arancia was how one would order a glass of orange juice. Fortunately for most diners, the picture menu was sufficient for ordering the specialties offered nightly, and wine was always vino. It helped to know which vino one wanted to experience with a specific dinner dish, but it was always safe to let the mater d' recommend the wine, as they never misled you with anything that would not please the palate. As to décor, it was hard to judge exactly what color the walls were painted, the color of the carpet, or the exact design of the tablecloths because the lighting level in the restaurant was dim and at a very low level. Daphne would swear that she saw some violin cases that might be disguised as a hiding place for machine guns, but she often let her imagination run away with her. Daphne felt like she could close her eyes in this Fairhope restaurant and open them in Italy or Sicily. She knew she had a vivid imagination, and this was a great place for her to experience the fullness of her possibilities.

"Do you think you could have found a darker place for us to meet?" Clara complained to Daphne. I can barely see in front of my face, much less the menu or the wine glass."

"What do you think of Gambino's Klahan?"

"It definitely has a flavor all its own," he said and smiled. "We might discover that the person shooting at us is eating dinner with us tonight!"

"Such dramatics from you two," scoffed Daphne. "If someone is out to get us, and I'm still not sure that's the case, this is the last place they would try anything. Rumor has it that the owner of this fine establishment is connected to the New Orleans Mafia family. They never fight where they eat and where their families are involved. This may be the safest place for us to discuss all the events of the day. Now, both of you need to tell me what you discovered in your search for the truth about Mayor Jackson." Klahan volunteered to go first.

"Are you going to loop John in on this conversation?" Klahan asked just to remind Daphne that the only way John Bremen would be privy to their conversation was for Daphne to call him and put her phone on speaker.

"Not this time, and for two good reasons," Daphne answered. "First, I don't want John bothered by worrying about us being in the line of fire while he is confined to the Ashburn office recuperating. That would make him feel terrible. Second, when a cell phone is on and transmitting a signal the screen lights up, and in a room as dark as Gambino's dining area would be a red flag if anyone is surveilling us. I will fill him in on what he needs to know once I am back in the Fairhope Inn later tonight." These comments were matter of fact, and nothing to be debated by anyone at the table, and Klahan and Clara knew it.

"That sounds reasonable," Clara said, acknowledging Daphne's complete authority in John's absence. John Bremen normally took the lead in giving directions and clarifying questions during an investigation, but he was not presently available to do so. Clara, Klahan, and Daphne knew that they would have to pull together to make this happen in John's absence. Besides a definite authoritative voice, John brought more experience to the Bremen and Whitacre Detective Agency than the rest of the team combined. However, they would have to soldier on in this case, because by the time John was well enough to rejoin the investigation there could be more collateral damage, more deaths of innocents, and suspects disappearing and going underground. That would be especially true if one of the five Mafia families was involved in any way with what was happening. And, if John had been present at this point in the investigation, he might boldly meet with one of the Mafia's top people to give them a chance to disavow their involvement in any of these murders and the attempted assassination on himself. John had done that before when he was in charge of the Dallas F.B.I. Office. It had worked, at least it had given clarity to the Mafia's involvement. John had learned over the years that the Mafia was lots of things, but they rarely lied about their involvement in specific crimes. They might skirt the issues, but John had never experienced a Don or Consigliere outright lying to him. The mob had too much pride to believe that they had to hide behind anything, and they always believed that they had the power to pull off the things that they had planned. Klahan, being a foreign national, and Daphne being a woman, would not get to first base with anyone in the Mafia when it came to a face-to-face meeting, should one be agreed on by both sides. The only foreign nationals that the Mafia recognized having authority were Italians and Sicilians, and women were to be protected, make babies, and keep their eyes open and their mouths closed. It was an eternal code of the Mafia—from Sicily to New York, and from New Orleans to Miami. Dating back to the 19th century, during the reign of the Bourbons in Naples, and transitioning from feudalism to capitalism, the Mafia had been around for almost two-hundred years, in some form or another. The nobility owned most of the land and had their own private armies to enforce their authority. It has been suggested that the birth of the current day Mafia came from those conditions in Italy and Sicily at that time. Actually, according to Wikipedia, "Ndrangheta was the original Mafia family and was established in Calabria, Italy, in the late 18th century, and it was alive and well in many European countries, as well as the United States at the present day." While it only boasted of about 6000 members worldwide, it was very lethal and effective when racketeering, drug trafficking, loan sharking, weapons trafficking, money laundering, fraud, extortion, murder, robbery and kidnapping was employed by the organization. When it originated it was created to protect the interests and assets of the large landowners in Italy, but now the organization was worldwide, and one of the most dangerous criminal families in the world. Just a few years ago, members of the Gambino and Bonanno families were arrested and implicated in criminal activities associated with the original family organization. It was reported that the annual revenue of the 'Ndrangheta family exceeded $50-60 billion, or about 3 ½ % of the GDP of Italy. In other words, this crime syndicate was not going away, and getting along with them was the best option for survival in Italy, as well as other places on the worldwide scene. Everything Mafia related in the Southern United States was masked by facades that gave the organization a look of respectability. However, one thing that John and Klahan knew firsthand. The Mafia's main goal was obtaining money and power, little petty disagreements were not usually part of a vendetta issued by a mob family. Therefore, if the Mafia was involved in the murders of Larry Washington and Jim Edmonds, as well as the attempted murders of John Bremen and Klahan Chu, it had to do with money or power. So, following the money, as Harry Lawrence had suggested to Daphne earlier in the day, was a good bet to lead them to the real cause of any involvement the Mafia might have in the affairs of Mayor Jackson and the City of Fairhope. It could also exonerate the mob from any suspicion of involvement in any of this City of Fairhope mess. The water had become muddy, and what Daphne, Klahan, and Clara needed right now was clarity.

"I'm going to call John from my secure cell phone when I get back to the hotel, and we will discuss moving forward with this investigation. I know John will not want to shy away from anyone trying to kill him and Klahan, so we will simply need to come up with a direct way to speak to the Mafia to see what involvement that they might have with Mayor Jackson and the Rocky Creek Golf Club. I want to see how John suggests we approach the mob on this one."

They received their dinners, ate in mostly silence, and finished in less than an hour. They decided to walk back to the hotel in two groups, protecting their ability to carry the investigation forward if one or more of them was attacked by an unknown source. They all safely arrived back at the Fairhope Inn, and each went to his or her respective rooms.

* * *

Daphne had gotten a shower, propped herself up in the canopy bed, and made the call to John. He picked up on the first ring of the cell phone.

"Daphne?" John asked with a worried tone to his voice as he addressed her. "What's going on down there? I was getting worried about you and the team. Is everything OK?" Daphne hesitated to answer John's question, which prompted another more direct question from him. "Are you, Klahan, and Clara alright? I had a feeling that the heat might have been turned up on the object of our investigation, and I imagined more fireworks. Tell me I'm worrying for nothing."

"Sorry, John, I can't do that." Daphne recounted the shooting at the Lucy Ledbetter Detective Agency Office, Klahan's near death experience, the findings of Clara and Klahan on tracing Mayor Jackson's money and investments, and their just completed dinner at Gambino's Restaurant. John was quiet for a while, and Daphne could image John's brain operating in overtime to put two-and-two together. He was a master at cutting through the fog of the moment, the facts unrelated to the ultimate answer being sought, and eventually determining a precise plan to accomplish the overall goal. Daphne hoped he would not fail them this time, because she had just about run out of ideas on this investigation. John suddenly spoke authoritatively, and Daphne was encouraged that he had been thinking of a foolproof plan of action, or at least she had hoped so.

"It looks like the Mafia may have reared its ugly head once more in our investigations. One thing we know about the Mafia, Daphne. They are mostly interested in establishing power and acquiring monetary payments from those they victimize. I do think that Harry Lawrence was right to focus on following the money trail. That usually leads to more questions or the answer to questions that end the search. In this case, if someone knows that Clara and Klahan are our investigators looking into the financial dealings of Mayor Jackson, and if Jackson is connected to the mob in some way or the other, then we will know quickly. The Mafia will move to protect their own, or they will abandon anyone who might be trying to implicate them in something in which they have no participation. Either way, we need to make them aware that we are watching and need to hear which side of the fence they sit."

"I guess it couldn't get much worse than shooting you, shooting at Klahan and Clara, and possibly coming after me. What's our next move?" John thought for a moment before he spoke, then he simply said "the highest level of exposure you can give any financial misdeeds you discover on the mayor and his cohorts. That will bring out the true enemy."

"Do you suggest how we go about doing that and remaining alive?" Daphne chuckled at her question, but John knew she was serious and answered her accordingly.

"You need a surrogate to leak the info to the local news agencies and television stations. The question is how to present it to them in such a way that they don't know you are the one providing the information. One tried and true way is to send an inquiry to their best investigative reporter and not suggest they do anything with it. Otherwise, they may think it's a setup and will stay away from exposing it to their local audiences. What you need is peer pressure on the mayor to prod him into showing his hand."

"And if he is not the guilty party, or is not somehow involved in the murder plots?"

"Then you will discover that you are pursuing the wrong person and you will be able to narrow your investigation once more. Who else is on the radar down there who could be implicated in any of the murders or attempted murders, other than Mayor Jackson?"

"The only players whom I think might be involved are Gary Tillis, the golf superintendent; Colonel Rocky Crawford, the Fairhope Police Chief; and possibly some unknown Rocky Creek Golf Club member yet to be identified."

"How much background checking have you done on Crawford and Tillis?"

"Just routine stuff. What are you thinking?"

"If we do a similar workup on those two that we did on Mayor Jackson we might find some interesting facts that could generate more leads."

"Good idea. Let's get Klahan and Clara on it. Also, why don't you get Clara and Klahan to compile a summary of the accounts that are questionable that they uncovered. Individually, it might not mean anything. However, together they might add up to substantial leads for us." Daphne agreed with John, and she told him that once she, Klahan, and Clara put everything together that they would have a conference call making sure everyone was on the same page moving forward. He hung up satisfied that his agency was operating just fine with him confined to the office. Clara and Klahan knocked on Daphne's hotel room, and she checked the peep hole in the door before she opened it.

"Come in," Daphne said, looking up and down the hallway to make sure no one had followed them to her room. "I just got off the phone with John, and we have a loosely-conceived plan to flush out the real culprit in these shooting. John is not convinced that the mob is involved in the shootings, because he said unless it concerns their personal money or an ability to grow or maintain their power the Mafia doesn't have a track record of getting involved with local crooks. As he once said to me when we were still with the F.B.I. in Dallas, 'The Mafia eats local tough guys for breakfast, and by noon they are no longer a threat to their empires!' Do you remember John saying something like that, Klahan?" Klahan smiled and nodded his head. Clara was looking pensive and asked a very pertinent question of both of them.

"If it's not the Mafia who has their claws into the mayor, who might it be? The C.I.A. or the N.S.A?"

"John also pointed out something that we need to consider when looking at the mayor for the murders of Jim Edmonds and Larry Washington. We simply can't put all our money on the mayor being the cause of the shootings, even if he is complicit in money laundering or other federal crimes."

"Good point, Daphne," Klahan said. "There is a lot of smoke coming from the mayor's area, so I just assumed he was the bad guy."

"He very well may be the bad guy, or someone may be framing him." Clara and Klahan looked at her as if she had two heads.

"Really? You think the mayor is on the up-and-up?"

"I never said that Clara. I just am redescent to put all our investigative energy on the mayor when we haven't looked into other possible people involved in the Rocky Creek Golf Club or the City of Fairhope."

"Anyone in mind?"

"Well, let's see. There's Colonel Rocky Crawford, the Fairhope Police Chief. And, then we have Gary Tillis, the golf superintendent. Follow my thinking for a bit. The Fairhope Police Chief had the opportunity and means to eliminate Jim Edmonds, assuming he had a definite motive. The same can be said for Gary Tillis. One of the murders happened on his watch on his golf course links. Why not consider them as well?"

"I can see the possibilities," Klahan said. "What do you want me and Clara to do about gathering information on these two potential perps?"

"John suggested that we do an 'in depth' background search on them, and not the simple credit and driver's license searches. Klahan you can do your thing with the F.B.I.'s possible files, and Clara can do a thorough financial picture on both of them. I hate to think a person who has been hired by the community to serve and protect has suddenly gone bad and broken the very laws he was hired to defend, but stuff like that happens. Can you both get some results by tomorrow afternoon?" They both nodded their agreement. "OK, we will make a conference call with John tomorrow around 2:00 PM. Come here and we will use my dedicated secure line on my cell phone for that conference call." They all agreed, and Klahan and Clara went to their rooms to get a good night's rest. When Daphne looked at her watch she saw that the hour had just passed midnight.

* * *

No one in the Bremen and Whitacre Detective Agency slept well that night, and morning just brought more questions that needed to be addressed. Running a simple credit and background check had not sent any red flags on the police chief or the golf course superintendent. Everyone knew about the three major credit bureaus that kept routine information about one's credit worthiness, but few knew that the federal government could track almost every financial transaction by using one's social security information, bank routing numbers, and other clandestine operations. Also, few knew that the F.B.I. and many other three-letter government agencies kept active files on many

Americans, whether it was legal or not. Generally speaking, the more visible and important a person might appear to the general public, the more likely the F.B.I. was acutely aware of the goings and comings of that person and all of his private financial dealings. An insider for the F.B.I. once stated that the agency was much like a Boy Scout—prepared when action needed to be taken. The real danger with such attitudes within federal agencies was that they monitored and disciplined themselves. Anyone could see the potential flaw in such logic. In this particular instance it was beneficial to Klahan and the Bremen and Whitacre Agency. Within a few hours of his request being made to a friend of his in the Dallas F.B.I. Office, Klahan knew more about the two men in question than they probably knew about themselves. Clara was able to gather local information that supported Klahan's findings, and now they needed to speak to Daphne to determine where to go from here. She agreed to meet them at a local coffee shop near the Fairhope Inn to discuss their discoveries.

"What did you two turn up?" was Daphne's first question of both her detectives. Daphne was thrilled that they might have turned up significant information in a matter of hours, and she wanted to plug that new information into the investigation results and see if any picture became clearer as to the perp's identity. Klahan went first.

"Both persons of interest have more financial investments than one might consider a small-town police chief or grounds keeper might possess. Crawford has stock in the Rocky Creek Golf Club, as well as some financial instrument that pays him a healthy monthly stipend that is directly deposited into a bank account in his name. I didn't see anything that indicated that he had any offshore accounts, nor did he appear to have suspicious income appearing and disappearing in and out of his bank accounts. Based on my initial investigation, I don't think Colonel Rocky Crawford is dirty, or at least not at level that we would see if he were involved in major money laundering or worse. Clara may have found more, but you'd have to ask her." Daphne looked at Clara as if to ask her to comment on Klahan's suggestion.

"All I found was some money that the police chief has hidden from prying eyes in a blind trust, but there's nothing illegal about that. I discovered that Colonel Crawford had those funds in his active accounts before he was elected to public office about ten years ago. It was quite a large sum, maybe a family inheritance or something like that, but nothing looked illegal about it. From what I saw the police chief can retire from work any time he decides he no longer enjoys his job. But, like Klahan's results, Crawford appears to be clean. He may be a little sneaky, but there's nothing illegal going on with his finances. Now, I can't say that about Gary Tillis the golf superintendent."

"Oh, how's that?"

"At a quick glance everything looks normal for a man earning a low six-figure income. As you may know, golf course superintendents earn a nice paycheck, and many of them drive nice cars and own exclusive homes on the fairways of the golf courses that they maintain. However, few of them have redacted files in their credit portfolio or police record."

"And I'm assuming from that last comment that Tillis does have redacted files?"

"Absolutely. If I didn't know better I would think his redacted files, along with Mayor Jackson's files, and recently deceased Jim Edmonds' files may have some things in common. We know Edmonds and Jackson were in the same military unit, and what if Tillis was as well?"

"That never crossed my mind."

"I hadn't considered it either until I did a little deep digging into Tillis' past. According to his military records Tillis was in the same unit as Jackson and Edmonds. He apparently was the last to leave the unit, but they all seemed to remain as friends, frequented the same golf club, and all had redacted military records. He also has sealed files from when he served on the board of a savings and loan company a few years ago. That particular lending institution went bankrupt, but Tillis was never implicated in foul play, even though he was a major shareholder and on their management board. The last tidbit of information may also surprise you. Tillis has part ownership in the Rocky Creek Golf Club. In fact, it appears he owns the same percentage of the club as does the mayor." Daphne asked Klahan if he had any supporting documentation that either proved or disproved the information that Clara had learned.

"Yeah, you might say so. According to the F.B.I. Office in Mobile, Gary Tillis was as culpable as Mayor Jackson and Jim Edmonds in whatever undercover work that they all performed. While I was being stonewalled by my official inquiry, Felicity Brown told me off the record that Tillis was considered armed and dangerous by their office. She cautioned me about getting too close to him without proper backup. According to Brown, people had simply disappeared when they got to close to Edmonds, Jackson, or Tillis."

"Do you think that Tillis is just acting as a greens superintendent, or does he have the expertise to do that job? I understand that the superintendent is the most important person on any golf course staff."

"You are correct about the importance of a good greenskeeper, and Tillis appears to be the real deal. However, his extracurricular activities in something illegal wouldn't have any impact upon his ability to perform his job at the golf club. If we are following the money, and that's what I understand our plan was from the beginning, then we have to determine how to see those redacted files. There must be something in those files that are key to our investigation."

"Do you think you friend at the Mobile F.B.I. will be able to help us with those redacted files without getting into too much trouble of her own?"

"Felicity's pretty savvy. I would bet that there are some gray areas, like workarounds, that she can do to find out enough information for us to be able to focus on whom the real bad guys are in these murders. Murder is something even the Mafia is careful about, because once a person has crossed that line things can only get more complicated. I think what we need to do now is try to determine *why* it was important to redact files on three civilians who once worked for Uncle Sam. That's the one common theme throughout all of the stuff going on down here." Daphne nodded that she was on board with Klahan's assessment of the facts as they knew them.

"How do you propose to move from suspecting to knowing that one or all of these guys were involved in something sinister?"

"I'm going to see if Felicity can give us the known third-party associations each of the three men in question have, how many of them are common associations, and if any of them have a grudge to settle. Sometimes people who believe that they have been slighted or cut out of a deal are less loyal than otherwise they might be. If she can come up with a common thread between Gary, Jim, and Todd, we may have something to work with."

"It's worth a chance," Daphne said. "What else can we do to move this investigation along? I feel we are getting somewhat bogged down in our approach to discovering what really happened at the Rocky Creek Golf Club, and the subsequent murder of Jim Edmonds may be just a distraction intended to throw us off course in our investigation of the golf pro's murder. By the way, did we do a background investigation on Larry Washington? I'm not sure it will make a difference in the long run, but we need to have all the facts possible to use deductive reasoning in this case."

"That makes sense," Clara said. "I'll run a standard background check on Larry Washington, and I'll keep you and Klahan in the loop. In the meantime, maybe you and Klahan can determine all the business interests Mayor Jackson may have in the area. We don't know those facts either." Daphne agreed to split up the tasks according to Clara's suggestion, and she and Klahan began checking with the local Chamber of Commerce, banks, and real estate companies.

“It the mayor has property and investments locally that might influence his actions from a business point of view, we need to know about it,” Daphne said.

“I agree. Why do you and Klahan compile the known assets of the mayor, the late Jim Edmonds, and Gary Tillis, and we can meet to discuss it after dinner.” They all left and focused to get their particular tasks completed as soon as possible, and, hopefully, before anyone else died mysteriously.

It was getting late in the afternoon, so Clara thought a trip to the Chamber of Commerce might be the best use of her limit time to work during business hours. She suspected that any inquiry she might make at the City Hall could alert the mayor that he was in the cross hairs of their investigation. She would start with the Chamber, go to the banks and savings and loan companies in the morning, and finish off with the commercial real estate brokers after lunch tomorrow. She would leave the electronic snooping up to Klahan. That type of thing was in his wheelhouse.

Klahan had placed a call to Felicity Brown when the small meeting had finished, and he saw that his cell phone was indicating that the Mobile F.B.I. office was making a callback to him. He answered the call as if he didn’t know who might be calling.

“This is Klahan Chu. May I ask who’s calling?”

“Klahan, this is Felicity Brown. I think you and I may want to sit down and speak together, but I don’t want to say too much over the air on a cell phone, if you know what I mean.” Klahan smiled to himself, because Felicity’s reluctance to speak to him about the issues he had raised about the three Fairhope friends was beginning to look important.

"Sure Felicity. Why don't we have dinner, and we can talk at that time? There is a small Italian restaurant near the Fairhope Inn where we can meet without being spied on or listened to by prying ears. Are you familiar with Gambino's Restaurant?" Klahan could hear Felicity chuckling at his suggestion.

"Did I say something funny?"

"I'm not actually laughing at you, Klahan. I'm laughing because you picked a restaurant that we have had staked out in the past numerous times when surveilling potential criminal elements, like the Mafia. It would not surprise me if there were an active Mafia family that had part ownership in Gambino's."

"Would you rather meet some other place?"

"No, Gambino's perfect. By the way, do you suspect the mob is involved in the murders that you're investigating?"

"I would be surprised if they were involved in any way. When we meet tonight I'll fill you in on what we know, and then explain what we need to know to clear up this case. Is 7:00 PM good for you?" Felicity agreed on the time for the meeting and hung up. Klahan had just enough time to freshen up and change clothes before he met Felicity for dinner.

Chapter 16

The Revelation

Daphne called John at the office to give him a summary of what his detective team had been doing to bring this case in Fairhope to a close. Julie Anderson answered the office telephone and said she would transfer the call into John's office. Daphne didn't have to wait very long to here John's voice.

"Daphne?"

"Yes, John. It's me. How are you feeling this afternoon?"

"Bored," was the only thing he said when he answered her inquiry.

"I called to bring you up to date on what we've been doing down here. I think you'll be pleased with our progress to date."

"I'm listening. Tell me something good. I'm bored out of my mind just sitting here trying to keep busy."

"We discovered that Gary Tillis, the golf course superintendent served in the same military unit as did Jim Edmonds and Mayor Jackson. His files in the F.B.I., as well as some local financial data, have been redacted in an identical way to Mayor Jackson's and Jim Edmonds' files. Also, we discovered that he owns an equal amount of stock in the Rocky Creek Golf Club as does his friend, Mayor Jackson. We don't have all the information back on Jim Edmonds, but it wouldn't surprise me if he hadn't owned stock in the golf club as well."

"In summary, what do we know for sure?" John asked.

"It appears that all three men, the mayor, Jim Edmonds, and Gary Tillis, were the controlling partners in the Rocky Creek Golf Club. Clara is looking into the possibility of Larry Washington having owned shares of the golf club as well."

"And the AK-47? What part does it play in all of this?"

"So far, nothing at all. That's what's weird. I'm beginning to believe the gunman meant to either only wound or scare you, and they used an old Cuban relic to throw us off track in our investigation. It appears to me that this may be simply a grab of greed and power by the remaining members of the Rocky Creek Golf Club. I'm not sure yet, but you and I know how the mob works, and if they were out to kill you or any of us they would have succeeded."

"See what Klahan and Clara can find out about Larry Washington. I know he was a golf professional, but what else do we know about him? Did he live locally, was he a member of the Rocky Creek Golf Club, and did he have any ownership in any other local businesses? The answer to those questions may help us begin to determine what really happened down there."

"That's a good idea. Do you really think that a golf course superintendent has the moxy to play in the same league with Jim Edmonds and Mayor Jackson? They appear to be pretty big hitters."

"At this point I can't assure you that I know any more than you, Klahan, or Clara. However, I'm a little farther away from the immediate area, and maybe I can see more of an association than the three of you. It's just a guess, but a guess founded on good assumptions."

"We'll check it out. Any other thoughts on the information that I have shared with you?"

"Not yet, but I'll give it some thought. Also, I'm gong to have Julie do a little telephone investigation from our end here in Ashburn. It never hurts to have more eyes on a paradoxical problem!"

"I agree. I'll get back with you as soon as I have more to report. By the way, have you heard any rumblings from Mayor Jackson about our getting too close to his protected secrets? He hasn't threatened to pull the plug on our investigation, has he?"

"He's too slick for that to happen. We still have lots of money from the initial escrow payment for expenses, and I doubt he will want to rescind an investigation that was initiated to clear him and his golf club. If he makes such a request, you'll be the first to know!" Daphne thanked John, reminded him that he was still recuperating from a serious health condition, and told him that she would call him the next day to keep him in the loop. She hung up and began to worry about her husband and partner of many years. They had been inseparable since they had met in Denver, when she was with the Denver Police Department, and he was with the F.B.I. It just didn't seem the same without him by her side.

* * *

Klahan arrived at Gambino's Restaurant a few minutes early to secure a quiet table in a dark corner of the restaurant for his visit with Felicity Brown. Using snitches was nothing new to Klahan but getting information directly from another F.B.I. agent was a little unusual, and Klahan wanted to make sure Felicity felt secure in the knowledge that he would not reveal his source of information under any circumstances. Of course, Felicity didn't really know Klahan, and the cover of a mysterious restaurant with dimly lit dining areas was about all he could do to put her mind at ease. He was sitting in a booth in the rear of the restaurant when he saw Felicity enter Gambino's. Klahan had instructed the maître 'd to direct Felicity to his table when she arrived. Klahan couldn't help but notice what a handsome woman she was as she walked toward the booth.

"Good evening," Felicity said as she waited for Klahan to rise as she slid into the booth. "This is a pretty shady looking place inside," she chuckled.

"Yes, but I doubt anyone will be paying us much attention while we are here. John and Daphne seem to think that some Mafia transactions may go on here, but I like the atmosphere. It reminds me of some of the places in New Orleans and Dallas where John and I investigated some of the Mafia Capos in those fine cities. We had a major takedown in Dallas several years ago, and the restaurant involved was in Dallas and was named Campisi's Egyptian Restaurant. It seems that Joe and Sam Campisi were connected with the mob back in the 1950s when the restaurant was bought by the two brothers. As you probably know, Dallas had one of the five major crime families headquartered there, and it wasn't unusual to see Capos and Underbosses at Campisi's on a regular basis. I've been told that even Jack Ruby was a regular at Campisi's, and that Joe and his wife visited Jack Ruby in jail on November 23, 1963, before he shot Lee Harvey Oswald on November 24,1963. Jack had owned the

Carousel Club in Dallas prior to the shooting of Oswald, and his association with members of the Piraino Crime Family was well known."

"I had read about you and John Bremen and your exploits in the takedown of several members of the Mafia in Dallas, Denver, and New Orleans. I guess that wasn't just bluster!"

"Nope, it was anything *but* bluster. There were some scary times back then. That's why I wanted to speak to you on a personal basis. I know how the Soldiers, Capos, and Underbosses work in the Mafia family hierarchy. They have no compunction to killing anyone who stands in their way of attaining their ultimate goals of control or monetary gains that they have established in their territories. However, one thing I have learned over the years when fighting the Mafia, they never seem to go after someone without a good reason—a motive. Either their target person has tried to impede their illegal collections and extortion, or they have a vendetta against someone because of the death of a mob family member that needs to be answered in kind. However, just to kill someone for the sake of killing them has never been evident to me of any of the families, and I've investigated Mafia families from Miami to New Orleans to Dallas."

"And you have reason to believe that code may have changed recently?"

"Someone took a shot at John a few days ago with a Cuban AK-47. It was one that has been traced back to the Bay of Pigs invasion in the early 1960s. According to what I have been able to discover, the Mafia wound up with most of those weapons and probably still own them today. If that is the case, why would a Mafia Soldier go after John

Bremen? What's the motive? Was it a rogue action from someone trying to settle a personal score?"

"I see why you might be confused about a motive, especially if the AK-47 actually did belong to the Mafia. I'm assuming you don't know that for a fact."

"Correct. We're just trying to put a logical motive together for the attempted assassination of John and two other murders that appear to be muddled by redacted information in those guys' historical files. It appears either the C.I.A. or the F.B.I. may be involved in trying to keep the missions that these persons of interest for us made in Afghanistan unknown for a particular reason. Of course, national security is the first thing that is mentioned when trying to get redacted information unredacted, but we have reached a dead end without help from the inside."

"You think I may be able to get that information for you? Legally or illegally?" She smiled when she asked the question. She had a nice smile.

"You tell me?" Klahan said, returning Felicity's mega-watt smile. "What we need to know is whether or not a couple of people whom we are investigating are dirty pertaining to business investments. We have no interest in what they did for the government or anyone else that could pose a security threat. However, we have three or four people who hold the majority ownership control of a well-known PGA golf course, and we need to know if there is more to it than them just putting out the money to purchase that controlling interest. There have already been two murders of these owners, and we need to know if there are national security reasons for that happening. Is that too much of an ask?" Felicity didn't answer for a moment, but

Klahan could see that she was thinking about what his request would entail.

"I tell you what I will do. You give me the four names that need researching, and I will get as much from their files as possible. I'm not promising anything, but I'll try."

"Fair enough. If you are able to help us, I'm sure John and Daphne would love to reward you with a Caribbean cruise, or something else that can't be traced back to you personally." Klahan handed Felicity a written list of names which included Mayor Jackson, Gary Tillis, and the late Jim Edmonds and Larry Washington. She didn't look at the list but slipped it into her purse to view at a later time.

"That would be nice, but let's not get the cart in front of the horse. It may take a couple of days for me to sort things out, but I'll do what I can. I can't put my job or my life in jeopardy, but there are ways to decipher information without knowing exactly what is in the files. There are far too many people being protected by the government for things which they should have been prosecuted for had their actions been exposed to the public. No one has the right to trample on other people's rights in the name of national security. You may be correct, or you may not be, but I will help as best as I can."

"That's all anyone can ask. Thanks!" Klahan and Felicity ordered their food, ate in relative silence, and then parted without a handshake. If anyone were watching them, Klahan didn't want this meeting to look anything other than it was—a simple meeting of acquaintances. Klahan began his walk back to the Fairhope Inn and Felicity got into her unmarked car and drove away. Now that the seed was planted, Klahan and the other team members needed to give it a little time to grow. When Klahan arrived back at the hotel, he asked if Clara and Daphne might meet him in the lounge for a nightcap.

"What did you accomplish with Felicity?" Clara asked. She had not been very successful with her initial investigation of the three Rocky Creek Golf Club members. No one in town was going to say anything negative about the mayor or any other prominent member of the golf club. Clara was hoping that Klahan had had more success in his endeavor to get to the truth.

"I had a very interesting dinner with Felicity. She would not commit to anything, and that was not surprising to me, but she did say that she would look into the files of our four-principal people of interest and let me know what she discovered. I gave her a list of our suspects, and she took it without comment. I guess we'll discover soon enough if there is anything in their F.B.I. files to be concerned about."

"Clara, you didn't come up with anything questionable about any of the four people in question? No shady business deals or attempts to purchase or sell anything illegally?" Daphne asked.

"All I found was that between the four of those men about half the business of Fairhope is controlled by them. They either own controlling interest in the businesses, or they own them outright. If they pulled their money from them the entire town could collapse from a lack of funding. I wasn't able to determine if they owned equal shares of the businesses in question, or if one was more vested than another one. However, if what I did discover is fact then those partners still alive are much wealthier than before the first and second murder was carried out. It's beginning to look like murder for one of the oldest motives on earth—greed!"

"What does your gut tell you about all this, Daphne?" Clara asked. Having been a detective for the City of Cullman, Alabama, for many years, she always developed a hunch about such things. Her gut wasn't always correct, but she was correct more times than she was incorrect. Daphne pondered Clara's question and just shook her head. Daphne had no idea what her gut was saying, and that bothered her even more.

"It may be time to divide and conquer," Daphne said. "Let's get John on the phone and get his input before we make any other moves." Daphne called John and he picked up on the first ring. "Bored, are you?" Daphne laughed as she could hear the excitement in John's voice. It was 10:00 PM and he was still up and wired.

"I can't sleep, and I hope you are getting ready to tell me that you have a breakthrough in our investigation. I was thinking of coming down tomorrow and helping out."

"Absolutely not. We are making progress, and you can best help by listening to what we have discovered so far and giving us your advice for us moving forward. You need to stay put and get well. That's an order!" Klahan and Clara chuckled, and John was silent on the other end of the phone. He didn't like being told what to do, even by a pretty redhead.

"I'm really feeling much better," he said. "I can be of help to you all."

"You can be of the same help working out of the office in Ashburn," Daphne insisted. "I'm going to give you an update on what we know, what we suspect, and what we have done to bring things to a head in the investigation. What you can do to help the most is give us clarity moving forward. We may be too near the forest to see the individual trees down here." Daphne told John everything that they had learned from the F.B.I., the local businesses, and the thorough background checks. She also mentioned Klahan's visit with Felicity Brown and her behind the scenes intelligence gathering efforts. What Daphne wanted most from John was a suggested unbiased approach to moving forward.

"I'm assuming Clara and Klahan are listening into this conversation?" he asked. Clara and Klahan acknowledged their presence and sent their best wishes to their boss. "Daphne, you and I have used the Ben Franklin problem-solving technique before, and I think Klahan and I have done so in the past. This may be a new approach for Clara. As you know, some decisions are not that clear cut. There are reasons to do something, but almost as many to *not* do it. When old Ben had such a decision to make, he would take a piece of paper, draw a line down the middle, put a *yes* at the top of one side of the paper, and a *no* at the top of the other side. He would list every reason he could think of for both sides, then count up the lists. If there were more yeses that nos, he would go with his yes side, and vice versa. It sounds to me like you're down to two major suspects in the murders of Gary Tillis and Jim Edmonds. While there may be other possibilities out there, you are pretty sure either the mayor or the golf superintendent was complicit in both deaths. Correct?"

"That pretty much sums it up," Daphne said.

"OK. As strange as this may sound to you, I believe you need to choose one side or the other—the mayor or the golf superintendent—and go after the other one. Bring the less likely suspect in on what you're doing and see if he can help you find enough facts to clearly indicate that the other suspect is guilty. That would be my advice." No one spoke for a moment, and then they all nodded their approval of the idea.

"That's a good thought, John. We will give old Ben Franklin a shot. Thanks for your input, and you keep your butt in Ashburn. Do you hear me?" Daphne said.

"Yes, Dear," was the only reply that John could muster. Daphne wished John a good night's rest, and she hung up the phone. She looked at Clara and Klahan and they just seemed to stare back blankly at her. She understood their confusion. They would try the Ben Franklin approach, but each remaining partner at the Rocky Creek Golf Club seemed as dirty as the other one.

Chapter 17

Ben Franklin's Help

No one had to be reminded that Benjamin Franklin was one of the brightest minds of all times, and a great inventor and statesman. Those who had studied the inventor in depth knew Ben was also a very pragmatic man. He had a way to make difficult decisions that few could argue was not sound in its principles, if not always applicable to all situations. When this founding father couldn't see a clear outcome of a decision, he would take a piece of paper, draw a line down the middle of it, write a plus symbol at the top of the left column, and a negative symbol in the right column. He would then think of every positive reason he should make that decision, and then Ben would do the same exercise for all the reasons to not do the same thing. Once he had exhauster his mind on pro and con reasons to make such a decision, he would simply count the number of positive reasons to do it, and then add the negative reasons to not do it. Whichever side had the most reasons was the most practical decision. Simple, but effective, way to decide a difficult decision. Daphne and John had employed this method, the Ben Franklin Decision Making Process, many times over their professional careers. Daphne had to admit that one or more times this technique had betrayed them, but generally it worked. Therefore, she had no hesitation in using old Ben's technique of decision making in their current case in Fairhope. After explaining the Ben Franklin technique to Klahan and Clara, they began making their list of yeses and noes for their decision. Instead of yes or no as topics, they used the names of Gary Tillis and Mayor Jackson as to whom they would direct their most attention. When they had finished their personal deliberations, the overwhelming decision was to target Mayor Jackson as the suspect in the murders and other happenings that were taking place in Fairhope. However, Daphne cautioned Klahan and Clara that Ben wasn't always correct. She wanted them to keep an open mind that the greens keeper could still be complicit in the murders they were investigating. Something in Daphne's gut told that Gary Tillis was not guiltless in everything that had transpired in Fairhope. She currently had no firm reason to draw such a conclusion, but her gut had been right before!

"Clara, I want you to investigate every financial asset that the mayor is invested in, and I want to know how much control he has in each of those assets. Also, we need to know who else has an interest in the same assets, the amount of financial liability each person has, and who stands to lose the most if that particular asset is forfeited. What we need is a better financial picture of the mayor's assets. Would he benefit greatly with Larry Washington and Jim Edmonds out of the way? I don't think we can get a handle on things until we know those things. How long do you think it will take you to discover those things?" Clara speculated silently momentarily and then answered as truthfully as was possible.

"It appears the good mayor has a financial interest in just about everything of value in the Fairhope area. It will take at least twenty-four hours or more to run all that information to ground."

"OK. Let's meet back here at the hotel in the restaurant tomorrow evening around 6:00 PM. Will that give you enough time to do what we need to get done?"

"I think I can manage it. Do you mind if I call Julie at the home office and get her involved in the routine background checking on Mayor Jackson?"

"I think that's a great idea. Just make sure she knows what she's looking for and how to approach the local businesses, so she doesn't spook them."

"Got it." Clara told Daphne and Klahan that she was going to bed and would see them the next evening at the Fairhope Inn restaurant unless something spectacular happened. They wished her a good evening, and Clara moved down the hall to her room.

"Klahan, while I have Clara and Julie researching Mayor Jackson, I want you to continue to see if Felicity can clarify just exactly what the relationship was between Mayor Jackson and Gary Tillis."

"What are you suspecting she will discover?"

"I have no idea, but something is not adding up. Why would a blue-collar worker, such as a greenskeeper, be keeping such close company with big shots like Jim Edmonds and Todd Jackson? Something doesn't seem right to me. Is there blackmail or some other type of leverage going on between the mayor and the greenskeeper? I may be just superstitious, but those two don't seem to be running in the same circles. You know what I mean?"

"Yeah. I've thought the same. Felicity said she would look into the redacted files on all four of our suspects—Jim Edmonds, Larry Washington, Gary Tillis, and Mayor Jackson. I hope to hear back from her tomorrow morning. You'll be the first person I contact when I have more substantial information to share."

Klahan excused himself, and he headed down the same hallway to his room where Clara had just disappeared. Daphne continued to sit in the restaurant trying to get everything lined up in her mind. What had seemed like a straightforward investigation just a few days ago had become as convoluted as any investigation Daphne could remember. She would get a good night's rest before starting over again in the morning. At least they had apparently narrowed their suspects to two people. How hard could it be drawing a logical conclusion at this point in the investigation. She hoped her thought process about these murders wouldn't betray her. It was then when her cell phone rang, and the identifying name on the phone surprised her, but she answered it anyway.

"Yes, Mayor Jackson. How might I help you?" Daphne was not prepared for what the mayor said. His voice was quivering, and his phone demeanor was anything but cool and smug.

"I'm in big trouble, Daphne. I need for you or one of your people to come to my home and speak to me tonight. Time is of the essence!" Without any more explanation the mayor hung up. Daphne stood looking at her phone in her hand as if it were a serpent or deadly spider. She was rarely thunderstruck, and this was so out of place for the distinguished, aloof Mayor Jackson. She called his cell phone back for an explanation, and Mayor Jackson answered the phone.

"Slow down, Mayor. Please start at the beginning of the story and don't skip any details in what has upset you." Although the mayor was obviously unnerved, Daphne could hear a little chuckle in his response.

“It’s not that easy, Daphne. Just suffice it to say that I believe my life is in danger. There are things so secret that I could never reveal to you, but I’ll try to tell you as much as I can tonight. I will say this one thing. It deals with National Security of the United States. There’s nothing much more I can share with you on an unsecured telephone line, but I’ll explain tonight. I will be home by 7:00 PM. Please tell me you will come, and you must come by yourself.”

“I’ll come tonight, but I will be expecting some real answers from you, and not just some runaround conversation. Do you understand, Mayor?”

“I promise to tell you enough to convince you that I’m in serious danger.”

“Seven o’clock it is,” Daphne repeated the time the mayor had requested,

He hung up again and Daphne decided that the mayor really believed that he was in danger, whether he was or not. She would need to speak to John before she met with Mayor Jackson, and she make a quick call to the office. John picked up on the first ring of the telephone, and Daphne was surprised that Julie was not manning the switchboard.

“Bremen and Whitacre Detective Agency,” John said. “How may I help you?”

“It’s me, John. Why are you answering the telephone? I thought that’s why we hired Julie!” She was kidding him, but she was curious at the same time.

“I’ve never been so bored in all my life, Daphne. I have got to get out of here and back into the field. I’m feeling fine, and the doctor has released me from my incarceration. How are things going in Fairhope? Have you guys figured out who the perp is yet?"

"How long do you think it would take you to get down here if you really tried?" There was a moment of silence on the call, and then John spoke with the authority that Daphne was accustomed to hearing from her husband, business partner, and best friend.

"Four hours by car or two hours by chartered plane. How soon do you need me?"

"It's 1:00 PM now, and we have an interview with Mayor Jackson at 7:00 PM. I think you can make it by car with time to spare. Do you feel like driving 250 miles as you're recuperating?"

"I'm telling you that I'm fine. I feel no pain, and I need to get out or I will go stir-crazy. I can leave here within the hour, so I should get there by 6:00 PM. Are you still at the Fairhope Inn?"

"Yep. I still have the room with the king-sized canopy bed. I'm sure I can make room for your overnight stay!" Daphne had a way of making every routine invitation sound sexy, and this was no exception.

"Do you want to give me a head's up before I get there?"

"I have a better idea. Have Julie lock up the office, and she can chauffeur you down here while you read all our notes. That way you will be up to date when you get here. She's helping Clara investigate this case anyway, and she can do that work from here as well as from Ashburn. How does that sound?"

“Sounds like a great plan!” Daphne could hear the excitement back in John’s voice—something that had been missing since she had had to send him home after being wounded while investigating earlier. “I’ll email all the updates to you so you can read them on your iPad on the way down. Hopefully, Julie prepared a ‘bug-out’ bag as we instructed her to do when she first came to work. I know you always have yours ready to go!”

“One way or the other we will be heading that way soon. See you when we get to Fairhope. I’ll text you when we get to Baldwin County so you will know we are close.”

“Great. Be careful on the way down. We have quite the opportunity to catch the mayor in a weakened position, so maybe we can get to the bottom of all of this cloak-and-dagger stuff.” Daphne hung up, and she was happy that John was on the way to help her with one of the most frustrating cases they had ever tried to solve. She thought it was a good time to check in with Klahan and Clara, and she wanted them to know that John was headed to Fairhope. She called Klahan first.

“Hey, Klahan. I just thought you might want to know that John is on his way to Fairhope to help us solve these murders.”

“Is he up for it so soon after being shot?”

“He says he’s about to go crazy just sitting around the office. In fact, he was answering the telephone he was so bored. I think the best medicine for him right now is for him to get back to work. Anyway, he and Julie will be here by 6:00 PM, and we will be making a call on Mayor Jackson at home at 7:00 PM for a little conversation.” After speaking briefly to Klahan, Daphne called Clara and filled her in on the news about John's return to Fairhope. She explained that Julie Anderson could work as well from the hotel in Fairhope as she could at the office in Ashburn, and she really didn't want John to make the long trek to Fairhope from Ashburn, a four plus hour trip, by himself. Daphne knew that she was being a little overprotective of John, but what were partners/spouses for? Daphne told Klahan and Clara that they would all meet in the dining room at the Fairhope Inn at 6:00 PM to discuss the case once John was available. Daphne had only a few hours to get her questions and thoughts together before they grilled the mayor about all the weird things that had been going on in Fairhope. She took out a legal pad and began making notes to assist her in the interview.

Chapter 18

Mayor Jackson

After making some notes and thinking about just how she planned to confront Mayor Jackson at their 7:00 PM meeting, Daphne decided she could afford a short nap before John, Klahan, Julie, and Clara met her for dinner at the Fairhope Inn. She didn't realize how tired she was until the clock on the nightstand woke her after a two-hour nap. She was groggy and a bit confused when she first arose, but after splashing water on her face and walking around for a few minutes she regained her composure. John was due at the hotel in less than an hour, so she decided to shower and freshen up for her husband and full-time lover. They had been apart for the first time in many years and Daphne wanted to snuggle close to him on his first night's return to her bed. After standing in the steaming water for twenty minutes, washing and drying her hair, and taking extra care to make up her face to perfection, she was ready for John's return. Instead, her cell phone rang, and an unidentified number showed in the display on her cell phone. Daphne answered anyway.

"This is Daphne Whitacre. How may I help you?" The answer came back swift and harsh, and the comment set Daphne back on her heels.

"No one can help him now. You need to go to Mayor Jackson's home immediately before the police get there. Once the police are notified the house will be sealed and you will not be able to enter." Daphne tried to ask who had been calling, but she wound up speaking to a dead phone line. She finished getting dressed, ran to her Crown

Vic, and sped to the address the mayor had given her as his home address. Mayor Jackson lived in the Rocky Creek Golf Club Estates, and the rear of his house faced the ninth tee on the golf course. When Daphne pulled up to the house there appeared to be no one home. There were no cars in the driveway, no vehicles in the garage, and the front door of the oversized mansion was standing open. Daphne pulled her Glock, chambered a round, and cautiously entered the foyer. She called out for the mayor or for anyone who might have been in the house, but no one answered her call. She began to clear the house, room to room, and found nothing amiss on the main floor. The kitchen, library, den, living room, and great room were all neat and tidy, so she began moving quietly up the winding staircase. At the top of the staircase was a large landing, with three hallways running off the main room. One by one Daphne cleared the seven bedrooms and four bathrooms located upstairs, and she still had found nothing of concern. She walked to the end of one of the hallways, and she was able to see the golf course tees and greens from the observation deck on the back of the house. It was then that she saw the body hanging in the gazebo. She rushed downstairs, her gun still in a two-handed firing position, and she made her way to the gazebo that was located in the rear of the lot. As she approached the white, decorative structure she saw that Mayor Jackson was hanging from the timbers by a rope that had been knotted with a hangman's noose. She approached the mayor and immediately saw the effects of the suffocation he had suffered from being hanged, as well as his broken neck which made his head lol to the side. She pressed her fingers to his carotid artery and felt no pulse. His skin was cool to the touch, and it appeared rigor mortis had already begun to set in. She knew that indicated that the mayor had been dead for at least an hour or two, and she had to wonder if the tip she had received on the telephone was from the murderer. Was it a murder? Did the mayor commit suicide, even after pleading for help from Daphne only a few hours earlier? The evidence she was viewing was not adding up to a suicide, but was it possible the pressure had gotten to be more than Mayor Jackson could abide? Daphne was careful to not contaminate the crime scene, and she pulled out her cell phone and dialed 911. She reported what she had seen at the house, told the emergency operator that she would not leave the scene until the police arrived, and she sat down in one of the rattan chairs that occupied the gazebo. She needed to call John and her detectives before their scheduled dinner meeting. While she was getting her facts straight in her head, she heard a siren, and figured a black-and-white patrol car had pulled into the driveway. She was not surprised to see two uniformed police officers, their 9mm pistols drawn, moving her way. Daphne remained in her chair, raised her hands into the air, and waited for them to approach.

"Are you the person who called in the incident?" the heavy-set cop asked Daphne. He was keeping his pistol and his eyes firmly on the redhead.

"Yes, I am. My name is Daphne Whitacre, and Mayor Jackson hired our firm to investigate the murders of Larry Washington and Jim Edmonds. If I may lower my arms I can show you some identification."

"Are you armed?"

"I am. I carry a Glock 19, as well as a snub-nose .38 caliber revolver in an ankle holster." The officers were both holding guns on Daphne, and they demanded that she surrender her weapons and identification to them immediately. She handed both pistols to them, butt first, and then her detective shield and identification license. They looked at the weapons, smelled them for possible fresh gunpower, and gave her credentials a detailed investigation. They handed her cred pack, as well as her weapons, back to her.

"Do you mind telling us what you are doing in Mayor Jackson's home?"

"My partner and I had a meeting scheduled with him for 7:00 PM tonight, but I received an anonymous telephone call a short while ago informing me that I needed to come here and check on the mayor. I found the front door to the house standing open, no cars in the driveway or the garage, and after clearing the house room by room, I observed a body handing from the rafters of this gazebo. I couldn't determine from the observation deck on the rear of the house exactly whom the victim was, so I walked down here and found the mayor's body as you are observing it now. I didn't touch anything in the house or the gazebo, so your crime scene integrity should be undisturbed." The officer whispered between themselves for a few seconds and then seemed to lose interest in the conversation.

"What crime scene?" the younger, skinny cop asked. "It appears to be a suicide to me. What do you think, Joe?" Joe, his overweight partner, nodded in accord that it appeared that way to him as well.

"You don't understand. The mayor was about to get some things off his chest in a meeting with me and my partner in just an hour, and now he's dead of a suicide? Doesn't that seem a bit convenient and coincidental to you?" Both officers looked at each other and just shrugged.

"Perhaps you didn't know our famous mayor too well, Detective. He was anything but loved by his peers and constituents. In fact, he may have been the most hated individual I have ever known. Maybe he was so unhappy not having any friends that he took his own life. At least, that's the way we are going to present it to the coroner when she arrives." Daphne was getting steamed at this cavalier approach to what appeared to be the murder of Mayor Todd Jackson.

"Who is your lead detective?"

"That would be Detective Norris Waters. Do you think I should call him?" Daphne just shook her head as she dialed the police department on her cell phone. When the desk sergeant answered Daphne's call she was all business.

"I need to speak to Detective Norris Waters. My name is Detective Daphne Whitacre, and I am at the home of the recently departed mayor." Daphne clarified a few things and then said, "Yes, *that* mayor! Now will you connect me or what?" Daphne had raised her voice a couple of decibels and the two uniforms began stepping back from this redheaded twister. After a very short span of time, it appeared that Daphne was speaking to someone in authority. She answered several basic questions, calmly agreed to stay at the mayor's house until Detective Waters arrived, and she sat back down in the rattan chair.

"We have all we need to make our initial report," Joe the cop said, "so we are going to leave. The coroner is on the way, so I guess you can wait for her, assuming you want to do that. It appears that you had nothing to do with his suicide." If looks could kill Daphne would have been locked up for the murder of two deadbeat cops! Sensing her disapproval of them, they slinked off toward their patrol car. Daphne breathe a huge sigh of relief to have them out of her presence. Daphne called Klahan, Clara, and John. They all joined in on a conference call and Daphne explained that they would need to delay their dinner until after 8:00 PM. She would text them when she headed back to the Fairhope Inn. She would also fill them in on what had happened when she saw them. As she was finishing the conference call, Daphne observed a handsome, plain-clothes individual heading her way from the back of the house. By now, the police had set up crime tape around the house and grounds, and there appeared to be a multitude of people wandering through the great house from room to room. Daphne stood as the man approached, stuck out her hand in greeting, and gave him a cheerful welcome.

"You must be Detective Norris Waters," Daphne said. She gave Norris a firm handshake and sat back down in the rattan chair. "I guess you may have some questions for me, right?" He gave Daphne his 1000-watt smile and said simply that he was there to get the facts. The coroner also came into the residence and headed for the gazebo. Dr. Juanita Haralson would normally have been in her office in Bay Minette, but she had come to Fairhope for a conference and decided to drop by the mayor's house before she headed home.

"Please tell me what compelled you to drive over to the mayor's home this afternoon? Did you know the mayor personally?"

"Personally?" Daphne pondered the question. "No, not personally, but rather professionally. Mayor Jackson hired our detective agency to investigate the murder of the professional golfer, Larry Washington, that took place a short time ago at the Rocky Creek Golf Club. One thing led to another, and the investigation became broader than just the incident with the golfer. Now, it appears that at least three persons, all having close relationships with each other, have met their demise. The thing that makes their deaths curious is that they were all friends and investors in the same country club and other businesses. The mayor called me earlier in the day in fear of his life. It appears those fears were well founded." Dr. Haralson walked up to the still hanging body of Mayor Jackson, pulled out some instruments from her medical bag, and began running some tests and taking notes. Except for briefly saying hello to both detectives she had said nothing since she had arrived.

"Dr. Haralson do you think you can give us a preliminary T.O.D. and C.O.D. for the mayor before you leave today?" Daphne asked. Juanita nodded her head but still did not speak. After a few moments of silence between all parties, Juanita began a systematic, detailed report of her early findings relating to Mayor Jackson's corpse.

"According to a dictionary's definition, '*Strangulation is defined as asphyxia by closure of the blood vessels and/ or air passages of the neck as a result of external pressure on the neck.*' Basically, compression in the neck leads to unconsciousness and death by causing a hypoxic state in the brain. Once the carotid arteries are damaged, cerebral ischemia, bradycardia, and hypotension can occur. In other words, strangulation is a very efficient way to cause the end of one's life."

"Can you determine from what you have seen here if the mayor hung himself, or if someone else may have murdered him and made it look like a suicide?"

"Good question, but I don't have an immediate answer for you. I will only know for sure when I get his body on the table and open him up. I hope to do that the first thing in the morning, and if you want to be there you are welcome to view the procedure." Dr. Haralson indicated for two uniformed medical personnel to take the body down from the gazebo, place it on a gurney, and take it to the coroner's vehicle. She turned, nodded to the two detectives, and disappeared back into the house to leave the premises.

"That is a woman of few words," Detective Waters said. "Now, let's get back to my question before she blew in and out of here."

"What was it that you wanted to know, Detective?"

"What I asked was what inspired you to come to the mayor's home to inquire anything of him. Didn't you and your agency have a professional agreement with him, and not a personal one?" Waters looked skeptical at Daphne as she prepared to answer his question. Anyone with any real perception could see that Daphne was getting miffed, because her face and neck were turning to the color of her hair—fire engine red!"

"Look, Detective. I don't have time to play your games, so either ask an intelligent question or butt out!"

"Do I detect some hostility on your part, Detective Whitacre?" This guy appeared to be picking a fight, and he had no idea that Daphne had had about all of his sarcasm which she was going to abide. She spoke quietly but firmly.

"Once again, Detective Waters, I'm only going to say this one time. My firm is investigating the first two murders that are linked to the Rocky Creek Golf Club, and unless you have some legitimate reason to detain me, I intend to get on with the business at hand. Otherwise, get out of my face and stay out of my business!" Daphne rose to her full height, picked up the folder she had brought with her to question Mayor Jackson, and headed back inside the house.

"Don't leave the area until we have had time to do some investigating and have cleared you from any suspicion of Mayor Jackson's murder."

"I thought you said it was a suicide. You best make up your mind, so you don't go around making a fool of yourself and the Fairhope Police Department." Daphne shook her head in disgust and continued to walk toward her car. It was becoming obvious to her that the Fairhope City Council needed to be brought up to date on what she and the agency had discovered about Mayor Jackson and the other members of the Rocky Creek Golf Club. There were more secrets in this small town than in the Pentagon! Daphne called John and told him to have everyone meet at the restaurant in the Fairhope Inn at 8:00 PM to discuss the events of the past few hours.

* * *

Daphne went back to her room and saw that John had arrived while she was at the Mayor's house. He had stretched out on the bed and was snoring lightly as he dozed. She realized how much she had missed him and was happy to have her husband and partner reengaged in the investigation. She was tempted to wake him to inform him of Mayor Jackson's death, but she knew he needed the rest after the four-hour trip on the highway from Ashburn to Fairhope, so she let him sleep until a few minutes before their scheduled meeting with Klahan and Clara. At 7:45 PM she gently shook him and awakened him. At first his mind was in a fog, and he wasn't sure where he was and why he was in a strange room.

"You've been asleep, John. You and Julie just drove down from Ashburn to meet with Klahan, Clara, and me. It's time for everyone to meet in the dining room, so why don't you wash your face, brush your teeth, and join me in the dining room. I'll go on down, and you come as soon as you're able." He agreed, got up and went into the bathroom, and began to get ready for the meeting. Daphne went to the dining room and found Julie, Clara, and Klahan waiting for her.

"I'm glad we could all meet like this," Daphne began, and her detectives began to look around sensing that something was not as they expected it to be. Daphne was usually direct, funny, and precise in her summations of cases. It seemed to Klahan that she was trying to evade telling them everything she knew.

"Daphne, where is John?" Klahan asked. "I thought he was joining us for dinner. You have news?"

"Yes, I do have news, but I haven't shared it with anyone at this point, including John. He is freshening up and will join us momentarily. Why don't we order some horderves and wine until he arrives?" Daphne motioned their server over to the table, ordered shrimp and crab cocktail, allegator tails, and a bottle of white wine.

"Allegator tails? Have you ever had allegator tails?" Clara asked.

"No, but I understand they taste like chicken!" Daphne said with a laugh. Everyone giggled and the tension that had existed between the four of them relaxed some. They saw John walking toward the table, and they all got up and gave him a big hug.

"Man, it's good to see you!" Klahan said. He slapped John on the back and pulled out a chair for his best friend of many years. Their friendship went back to the mid-1970s when John help Klahan escape the North Vietnamese's capture of the Saigon Embassy. They had been inseparable since that time. Klahan's friendship with John predated John's relationship with Daphne, and that was saying a lot.

"It's good to be back. One never knows how frail the human body is until that person is sidelined by a bullet. Fortunately, the wound was through-and-through, and now I'm ready to get back to work." John looked at Daphne and he could tell that she was avoiding eye contact.

"John is back with us, and he and Julie will operate from the hotel while we beat the bushes. He was reluctant to agree to my terms, but that's the only way I would let him back on this case," Daphne said with authority. "There's nothing wrong with his mind, but his body is still recovering from the shock of being shot. I am counting on each of you," and she looked at Klahan, Clara, and Julie when she spoke, "to help me keep a rein on him. He's a tough cookie, but no one is tougher than an AK-47 round traveling faster than the speed of sound entering the flesh on one's body. I'm counting on each of you to help me help him!" At that point she looked at John sternly, making sure her message was delivered.

"OK, OK, I'll behave!" John Insisted. Anything to get me out of the office and Ashburn for a while."

“Now that’s the spirit, John,” Daphne said, and she placed a big kiss on his lips. He blushed, the others laughed uncomfortably, but Daphne was unashamed. She loved her man, but she expected him to behave!

The waiter brought the wine, the allegator tails, and the shrimp and crab cocktail, along with sauces to dip them in. John did the honors and poured wine for everyone, and they began to munch on the horderves.

“I have some news for all of your ears. I’m glad we are all sitting down because this bulletin will knock you off your feet!” Daphne watched her team as she began to reveal the news about the death of Todd Jackson. “Mayor Todd Jackson was declared dead of his injuries from an apparent suicide hanging in his gazebo at his home this afternoon. I just left his house before I came here, and I spoke briefly with Dr. Juanita Haralson, the Baldwin County Coroner, about the C.O.D. and the T.O.D. She would not declare it was a suicide until she had him on the table and after a complete autopsy. She will be performing that procedure tomorrow morning at the morgue in Bay Minette, and I am asking John and Julie to be present to get the results for us. With two murders already tied to the Rocky Creek Golf Club membership, I’m not assuming anything until I hear it from the coroner. We all know Juanita’s work. She’s the best, and if there are any innuendos of foul play in the mayor’s death, she will detect them. The autopsy is at 9:00 AM, and I want you two there for the procedure. Any problems with that?”

John and Julie shook their heads, and Daphne began to lay out the plans for the remaining agency members. They needed to focus their efforts on Gary Tillis, the golf pro at the Rocky Creek Golf Club. Of the four people who were most like involved in whatever government secrets and cover up that had happened recently, Tillis was the only one remaining who might be able to shed some light on what had happened to Todd Jackson and his other friends. They had dinner, a few drinks, and then everyone went to their rooms.

* * *

Morning brought a beautiful, sunny day with cool breezes blowing over the peninsula from the Gulf of Mobile. Fairhope was the largest city on the waterfront of the Bay of Mobile, and it was located just a few miles south of Daphne, Alabama, both sharing U.S. Highway 98 as a tourist travel route from the Gulf of Mexico to I-10. The water appeared to be calm in the bay, and it appeared the City of Fairhope was going to have a spectacular weather day. John and Julie were on their way to Bay Minette to observe the autopsy of Mayor Jackson, so Gary Tillis was Daphne's focus at the present time. Daphne picked up her cell phone and called the golf course.

"May I speak with Superintendent Tillis?" A young woman said she would ring his office, and for Daphne to wait until she heard him pick up the line to speak to him. The phone rang several times, and then the call was rerouted back to the operator.

"Rocky Creek Golf Club. How may I assist you?" the same voice said again.

"I just called for Superintendent Tillis, but no one picked up. Is he at work today?" There was a few seconds of silence while the operator checked her calendar.

"I saw him earlier, but he may be out on the course inspecting the tees or greens. May I give him a message?"

"No, thank you," Daphne said. "Can you give me directions to the club?" The young woman asked Daphne where she was located and gave her step-by-step instructions as to how to get to Rocky Creek Golf Club. Daphne thanked her and hung up.

"Klahan, Clara, get your things, and make sure you're packing heat. We are on our way to the golf course. We have been royally paid for this work, and I don't want to leave it unfinished." Then, without another word, the three of them were out the door and headed for Daphne's Crown Vic.

Daphne had always driven a Crown Vic in her job as the Sheriff of Denton, Texas, back in the days when John was still with the F.B.I. She loved the roar of the huge, super-charged engine, the smoke-tinted windows, and the push bumper grille guard that was painted black and matched the color of the car. Big black oversized tires with small moon hubcaps and police interceptor rear suspension made the car appear invincible. With Daphne driving, her Crown Vic *was* almost invincible. John feared for his life every time he had to ride with her at the wheel of her "magnificent monster," as she referred to it. Fortunately, the Crown Vic had a 5-point seat belt configuration, much like a race car would have as standard equipment. John still wasn't comfortable with Daphne at the wheel. She drove the Crown Vic much the same as she drove her 240-Z car—fast and furious!

"Get in and buckle up," Daphne said to Klahan and Clara. "You two can flip a coin to determine who rides in the rear and who rides in the front." They flipped a coin, Klahan won, and immediately got into the back seat. "You won, Klahan. You can ride up front!"

"That's OK," he said. "It will be exciting enough back here." Clara had never been with Daphne when she was driving the Crown Vic, so she didn't understand what all the fuss was about. Once they were driving down U.S. Highway 98 at 70 MPH in a 35 MPH zone, Clara became enlightened.

"Aren't you concerned about the Fairhope constabulary pulling you over and giving you a ticket?" Clara asked in amazement.

"Nope. I have a special Alabama Governor's tag and they wouldn't dare."

They zoomed past cars and trucks which appeared to be following the speed limit, dodging in and out, passing on the right and the left of any vehicle that might pose an obstacle to their quick arrival at the golf course. Rocky Creek Golf Club Estates was located on the east side of Highway 98, and they barreled into the gates and sped on to the clubhouse at breakneck speed. Once they had arrived, Klahan and Clara unbuckled their seat belt and staggered out of the car.

"That was some ride, Daphne," Clara said.

"Just an average trip for me, Girlfriend!" Daphne said and high-fived her detective. Clara glanced at Klahan and observed that he was somewhat pale from the circus ride. "You guys follow my lead." Daphne, Klahan, and Clara entered the clubhouse and asked for the manager.

Chapter 19

Vanishing Evidence

John and Julie were sitting in the coroner's office at 8:45 AM the next morning in preparation for the autopsy. Before the procedure began, Dr. Juanita Haralson came into the lobby and greeted them, inviting them into her office for a cup of coffee and a short discussion.

"That's a great idea, Dr. Haralson," John said.

"Call me Juanita. We've been through enough carnage to be on a first name basis by now," she laughed. John chuckled as well, and Julie sat silently taking everything in as an observant trainee might do.

"You are still going to perform the autopsy this morning, aren't you?"

"I am, but I'm not sure you need to be there for the actual procedure. According to what Daphne asked yesterday, she wanted to know the T.O.D. and the C.O.D. Has anything changed in that request?"

"No, I'm sure that is all we need to know at this time. Why?"

"I was able to determine the T.O.D. last night before I place the body in the cooler. I was at the mayor's house at 5:35 PM, and according to my instruments, his T.O.D. was sometime between 1:00 PM and 3:00 PM. His body hadn't begun move into rigor mortis when we found him, so I am thinking his death was closer to 3:00 PM. Rigor mortis usually sets in from two to four hours after death, and there was no indications of rigor when I examined him at the morgue last night. Also, the C.O.D. was an apparent suicide by hanging, at first sight."

"What do you mean at first sight?"

"When one is asphyxiated from a hanging there are usually a few things that indicate that the death was caused by a violent snapping of the neck, the interruption of the carotid arteries, and things of that nature. Mayor Jackson definitely did not die of a hanging, suicide or not. He appears to have been choked by some very strong hands. His eyes indicated that his loss of oxygen and circulation took place over a few minutes, not instantaneously, which is what would have happened had he hanged himself. He was definitely murdered by someone, and I would be surprised if that person was not a bodybuilder or someone who works extensively with his hands in heavy mechanical labor. It's not easy to strangle a person, much less a full-grown man in decent physical condition. It appears at first glance that the mayor was in excellent condition, hence the deduction that whoever strangled him was stronger than average. You and your assistant are welcome to watch the autopsy if you want to, but I think I have related the information that Daphne was inquiring about."

"You're right doctor, we don't need to see the actual autopsy. Thank you for the information and please send a copy of the autopsy to our office in Ashburn for our files once it's completed." John handed Juanita his business card and she placed it on her desk. "Thanks, again, for the clarification on his T.O.D. and C.O.D." Julie and John shook Juanita's hand, and they left the morgue for their trip back to the Fairhope Inn.

*   *   *

As Daphne and her detectives entered the clubhouse, they looked around at the opulence presented there. The floor was a warm, dark hardwood, the walls were wooden panels of pecan, and the tables in the dining room were set with crystal, silver, and linen tablecloths. The few people who were in the club that morning appeared to be sipping margaritas, wine, or pink ladies. They could look out of the ceiling-to-floor plate glass windows overlooking the putting green and the distant tees and greens and see a spattering of people riding around in golf carts or hitting golf balls from various places in the fairways or greens. It was a beautiful, surreal site, knowing that at least three active members had been murdered recently, and the fourth suspect was somewhere on the course in a golf cart or utility vehicle.

"We need to see Superintendent Tillis," Daphne said, flashing her detective credentials to the girl on the reception desk. She picked up the telephone and called for the club manager to meet with the detectives. They waited a few minutes until they saw a well-dressed man in his forties approaching them with a big smile on his face.

"I'm Jay Doran," he said, offering his hand in welcome. "How may I help you today?" Daphne flashed her credentials once more, repeated that she needed to speak to Gary Tillis immediately, and waited for the response from Jay.

"Have you tried his office?"

"We tried a short time ago before we actually arrived. He didn't answer his phone, but the receptionist said he was here today, possibly out on the course. Do you have any way to page or call him?"

"Sure," Jay said confidently. "Mary, please page Mr. Tillis for these people, and tell him he needs to come to the clubhouse to meet with them. Now, if that's all you need, I need to get back to my office. We are expecting a large gathering tonight for dinner and I still have things to do." He offered his hand once more, shook everyone's hand firmly, and disappeared back into his office. They waited twenty minutes for him, but the page was never answered.

"Will you please direct us to his private office? Maybe there is some indication there where he might be." Mary was reluctant, but Daphne gave her one of her "don't mess with me kid" looks, and Mary showed them to Gary's office. They entered the office and noticed that the filing cabinet appeared to have been rifled through, there were broken glasses and other things scattered on the plush carpet, and some pictures that appeared to have been framed and hung on the wall behind Gary's desk were missing.

"Oh, my!" Mary said. She sat down and swooned at the apparent violation of Gary's office and personal things. "What happened here?"

"Mary, please go back to your desk and call the Fairhope Police Department. Ask for Detective Norris Waters. He is the Chief Detective, and he will want to come by and investigate what happened here. Please seal off this room and don't permit anyone to enter it until the detective tells you it is OK to do so." Mary left the office but was visibly shaking as she headed back to her desk. Daphne looked at Klahan and Clara and just shook her head.

“I don’t like any of this,” Daphne said. “I’ve seen this ending before.” She looked lost in thought, so Klahan asked her to explain her comments. “Someone or something has been one step ahead of us since our initial visit to Fairhope. In other words, someone doesn’t want us to solve these murders. I don’t know who, but I can guess.”

“It that a hunch, or are you basing it on facts?” Clara asked.

“Let’s say my experience in law enforcement for over twenty years, as well as my detective skills, are pointing to this being an unsolvable crime. In fact, I will be willing to wager either of you that John and Julie discovered that Mayor Jackson was murdered, and not a victim of suicide by hanging. Give him a call Klahan and see what they discovered in Bay Minette.” Klahan humored his boss and called John’s cell number. When he hung up he explained the T.O.D. and C.O.D. for Mayor Jackson. Daphne just shook her head and began to smile.

“What’s funny?” Clara asked.

“Big Brother has had a hand in this investigation from its outset. We were never going to solve these murders.”

“Don’t you think you’re being a little cynical, Daphne?” Klahan asked.

“Nope. In fact, why don’t you give your friend at the FBI, Felicity Brown, a call and see if there is any way we can have the records of those four men subpoenaed so we can try to unmask the redacted information. It all has to tie together somehow.”

"I think you're being paranoid, Daphne, but I will humor you." Klahan dialed the Mobile F.B.I. office and asked for Felicity Brown. He put the phone on speaker so Daphne and Clara could hear both sides of the conversation.

"I'm sorry. To whom did you want to speak to?"

"Agent Felicity Brown," Klahan said. A few minutes passed while the operator looked up Felicity's information.

"We don't have a Felicity Brown in this office. Are you sure you have the name right?"

"I'm sure. Will you please look again?"

"I'm sorry but we have all our agents listed on our electronic sign in board, and there is no Felicity Brown. I don't remember ever having a Felicity Brown in the directory. Would you like to speak to the director?"

"Please and thank you." A few more minutes elapsed, and a man's voice came on the line. I'm Phillip Green, Director of the Mobile F.B.I. office. How may I help you?"

"Yes, my name is Klahan Chu, ex-F.B.I. director of the Dallas, Texas, office. I need to know if you have, or have ever had, a Felicity Brown working out of your office as an agent?" The line was quiet for a moment and then Green responded.

"No, I don't recall that name, and I've been the director here for five years. Maybe she was here before I came, but no one by that name has worked here lately. Why do you ask?"

"I work for an investigative agency, and we have been retained by a prominent businessman in Fairhope, Alabama, to help determine what happened to a couple of people who have had a past with the F.B.I. I can give you their names if you will verify that you still have active files for them. I would be most appreciative."

"We don't normally divulge information of that nature, but I can tell you if we have a file for them. That wouldn't be breaking any kind of protocol."

"Thanks. The four names in question are Larry Washington, Todd Jackson, Jim Edmonds, and Gary Tillis. Even if you can't elaborate on the documents in their files, I just want to make sure you have files on them in case we want to petition the court to allow us access to them at a later time."

"I'll try the names in our data base." Again, the phone went quiet for a few minutes, and then Green returned once more. "I'm so sorry, but we don't have any files on any of those names. Are you sure about the spelling?" Daphne indicated with a finger gesture across her throat that Klahan should abort any more attempts to discover files on the four previous suspects who had been members of the Rocky Creek Golf Club. Klahan thanked Phillip for his time and hung up the phone.

"Now what?" Clara asked. She was obviously confused by everything she had heard at the golf course and from the Phillip Green.   Daphne began to laugh.

"Those sons-of-bitches!" was all she said. "Let's go back to the Fairhope Inn and prepare our final report for the Fairhope City Council." No one spoke on the way back from the golf course, and Daphne drove her big black machine at a decent speed. She seemed lost in her thoughts, so Klahan and Clara decided not to trouble her with any explanations. They figured she'd reveal what she meant when she was ready. They arrived back at the hotel, she called John and Julie and invited them to lunch, and they all gathered around a sun-lite table on the patio under the spreading Angel Oak trees. Everyone compared notes, and John gave Daphne a knowing look. She decided that now was as a good a time as any to explain what had happened to Gary Tillis, and all the other suspects, whom they had been chasing.

"John and I have experienced something of this nature in the past. When we were both police officers in Denver, Colorado, we were ghosted by a local municipal authority because we were getting too close to an undercover operation. We believe that's what happened in Fairhope."

"Ghosting? What the hell is ghosting?" Clara asked.

"The proper definition of ghosting is basically rejection without the closure. This often happens out of nowhere and can leave you feeling confused, hurt, and even weak. John and I think we were ghosted by the U.S. Government. For what reason, we may never know."

"You mean the F.B.I., don't you?" Klahan asked.

"Maybe," John said. "Klahan, you thought you were talking to the F.B.I., but maybe your weren't. This could have been an N.S.A., F.B.I., C.I.A.A, or some other three-letter undercover operation. Obviously, we don't know how sensitive the information we stumbled into is to whomever ghosted us, but people don't die in a small city like Fairhope, Alabama, disappear from a public golf course, or wind up murdered and disguised as having committed suicide. Daphne and I have decided to present a report to the City of Fairhope, and we will be heading back to Ashburn. You four can go on back and begin to put the office back in order for us, and we will be along sometime tomorrow. Be careful on your way home."

Though dumbfounded by the news and results of their labors for the past couple of weeks, the Bremen and Whitacre Detective Agency was going home, unfulfilled and with more questions than answers. At least they had been paid royally for their time.

Epilogue

John Bremen and his lovely wife Daphne had completed their written report which had been ordered by the late Mayor Todd Jackson before his tragic death. There were many details, questions that had been partially answered, and suppositions that could be drawn from the data collected from those parties involved with the unfortunate events that took place in the span of a couple of weeks in the quiet little town of Fairhope, Alabama. No one on the city council seemed surprised about the details surrounding the deaths of four prominent member of the Rocky Creek Golf Club. Actually, there were only three known deaths, and one missing person who never surfaced again after being spotted at the golf club early one morning. He just seemed to vanish into thin air, much like the supposed redacted files on all four men. Those files were never found as well. As John and Daphne were heading up Interstate 65 North toward Ashburn, John turned to Daphne who was manhandling the Crown Vic as if it were a Sherman Tank.

"Off the record, how do you really feel about the resolution, or lack thereof, in our last case?" Daphne didn't answer for a moment, but when she did she was succinct and accurate in her appraisal.

"I guess it's like kissing your brother, John." And nothing else was said for 100 miles.

www.ingramcontent.com/pod-product-compliance
Lightning Source LLC
LaVergne TN
LVHW041200150826
845673LV00001B/229

* 9 7 9 8 6 4 9 6 8 6 7 6 1 *